SPOILT AT CHURCH

FAGBEMI BOSEDE

FAGBLUMINOUS BOOKS

ISBN- 9798835461820

Cover design by: DEBORAH FAGBEMI

TO GOD, MY MAKER AND KEEPER.
I AM NOTHING WITHOUT GOD.

ONE

When Revd. Bamiro asked the worshipers to rise for the prayer at the end of the Bible study and the beginning of the prayer meeting, Kike saw an opportunity and jumped at it. Moving out of the auditorium, she prayed her Mum wouldn't notice her absence. Leaving the Church during a service was against her family rules and regulations for Christian living. It was considered a grievous sin. She knew what the consequence would be if caught. Even with that, the need to leave outweighed whatever punishment was in store for her. Therefore she took the risk and earnestly prayed that her parents wouldn't observe, especially her eagle-eyed Mum.

Kike hated Church midweek services. She hated Bible studies and prayer meetings. She didn't mind being at the choir practice; where she always had the opportunity of showcasing her talent, or the youth meeting; where she would be free to do whatever she liked without her parents watching her. Kike detested services involving her and the adults.

To her, Bible study was boring and depressing. She often questioned herself on what else she needed to know in the Bible. At age 17, she had read the Bible through three times. That was needed to qualify for various organizational requirements in the Church. She knew all the events in the Bible as she knew the palms of her hands and her name. Since she had represented the Church in countless Bible competitions and won many awards, she saw no new thing in the Bible that warranted adults being in Church every week to debate on and even tagging their innocent children along.

Kike envied friends whose parents weren't strict on taking

to Church for midweek services. Those were the busy types, or parents who didn't see the necessity of children being in Church. Kike would give anything to be in their shoes. Anything to be at home now watching a film, reading a novel or doing anything different from being at Church and pitying herself.

As she left the Church compound hastily, she almost collided with a friend - Martha, who was rushing to join the service. Both of them were Church friends who knew each other through the various organizations they belonged to, and their joint activities in Church.

Martha was a young girl of about age 16. She was of average height, caramel colored and slightly plump with an oval shaped face and deeply dimpled cheeks that always gave her smile a picture of innocence and shyness.

Kike was a direct opposite of Martha. At 17, she had the height of a fully grown adult. She was pole like and lean, with a characteristic way of walking that made it look as if she would break into two. The features, coupled with her long legs, always made her feel awkward and inferior. She seldom smiled. Both of them were emerging adults and final year students in the secondary school.

Accepting Kike's apology, Martha asked why she was in a hurry. "I need to catch up with someone," she replied. "By the way, why are you late?" She equally asked.

"Mum came back late from work. I was all along waiting for her, not knowing that she wouldn't make it to Church."

"You mean your parents are not here?"

"Yes! Dad is not in town."

"Then why are you here?"

"Because I want to be," Martha replied. "I like being in Church. Please let me go before I miss a good part of the prayers."

She left Kike standing and gaping after her. "Imagine her

coming for Bible study without being forced," she said. "I wish we could exchange parents."

Since she had lost time, Kike walked briskly, a little short of running. She turned to a corner and entered into a dark cluster of trees. Turning her head left then right, she moved into an uncompleted building where a lone man stood.

"What kept you long?" the man asked. He drew her towards him.

"Same old story," she replied.

"Your Mum?"

"My parents."

"I'm getting sick of this hide and seek game." He shrugged. I wonder why your parents are behaving like mother hens watching over their chicks. I prefer a girl with freedom; a girl that I can see at any time I want. There are countless girls that would give anything to be my girlfriends in the Church."

"Why are you talking like this?"

"To let you know that I might move on if things don't change."

"Please now Jide," she pleaded. "Please don't leave me. You know I love you."

"I know." He drew her closer. "Don't mind me, I love you too. It's just that I want more of you at all times."

"Yes! But we need a little more patience. Once I get into the University, I will have all the freedom in the world."

"That's my girl. Now! Let's have a quick one."

"No Jide!" Kike protested. She drew back from him. "Not today."

"Why not? I might not have the chance to be alone with you again for the next two weeks. As my only girl, you have to satisfy me."

"Today is not right. I don't have time to spare. There's also an issue I want us to discuss."

"What issue? I want you here and now," Jide insisted.

"Ha! We are having too much sex," Kike replied. "I'm beginning to feel guilty. We should engage in productive activities."

"Like? For crying out loud, when and how do we engage in productive activities? In the dark? In an uncompleted building? Do you have time for me? Maybe we should make babies as a productive activity. I will gladly ditch my condom if that's what you want."

Kike's heart sank at the mention of babies. Does he know? Is it obvious? Is it possible? "That is even…" she started to say, but he cut her short.

"Feeling guilty is not in the equation of love. Forget about what you hear, or what is taught in the Church. It's not easy for a relationship to survive without sex. You are just 17, with years before we could get married. Do you expect me to stay for those years without sex? It won't be possible. Lailai."

"We are choristers," Kike replied. We sing that fornication is not good. You are also a Sunday school teacher. Won't God get angry and kill us the way he killed Ananias and Sapphira because of their pretense?"

"That? God is a merciful God. If not, a good number of our Church members would be dead by now. See! I can bet you that 80% of   the youths in the choir are doing it. You talk as if fornication is the only sin God frowns at. There are bigger sins. Plenty!"

"I insist we reduce our intimate encounters."

Jide looked her up and down and turned his head in anger. "Why this talk sef? " He asked. "Is this the first time I'm demanding for it? Have we not had it at countless times? What is new? You were not a virgin when we first met? Were you not exposed before I had you? I knew the kind of challenge I would face by dating a Church girl like you; with your spiricoco mother and Deacon Father. Despite the hurdle, I threw caution to the wind and tamed my fear. I had the hope that I would meet you as a virgin."

"Please stop," Kike cried. She covered her ears.

"Stop what? The first misgiving I had about you was that, you gave no resistance to my love advances at the first trial. You fell cheap. So cheap. I was disappointedly surprised that your gate was without a barrier. Expecting to meet a narrow way that would lead me to paradise when I entered, I encountered a broad and worn out way. I pray you will not lead me to hell."

"Jide!"

"Anyway, keep your body and let me know where you want this relationship to lead to." Leaving her standing, he disappeared into the darkness.

Kike sank to her knees and burst into tears. "What will I do without you Jide? She whimpered. "Oh God! What will I do? He never cared to hear what I wanted to tell him." She stood and cleaned her face. Following Jide was out of context, except she wanted to get into a trouble that would further compound her problem. She brushed down her gown and ran to the Church, into the waiting arms of a visibly enraged Mum and a confused Dad.

TWO

Kike felt as if the ground should open and swallow her. Her initial plan was to sneak into the Church unnoticed, but here she is to the full glare of all and sundry, sweating like someone that just finished running a marathon. She walked past her parents to join her siblings in the car; weaving the story she would eventually tell them in her head.

Her parents were very active and committed members of Beulah Salvation Assembly. While her Dad was a Deacon, her Mum in addition to being a Deaconess was a strong member of the women fellowship and other Church organizations. The Pastor looked up to their family as role models and motivation for other families. Since the parents were well respected, it was expected of the children to be of impeccable characters. They must also live in accordance with biblical principles and doctrinal beliefs. Anything short of that was frowned at.

The Johnson's home was thus an extremely strict one; where the children were raised on laws that were meant to be obeyed and not be broken. There were laws on what to eat or not eat. Clothes to wear or not to wear. Places to go or to avoid. Friends to mingle with and how to behave, especially in the Church. The home was ruled with an iron fist by none else but Mrs. Johnson. Her husband was a gentle man who couldn't hurt a fly. He hardly spoke and when he did, you had to strain your ears to hear him. The children grew up thinking he was scared of their Mum.

They lived in perpetual fear of her koboko, deafening slaps and pinches that could make tears rush to their eyes with tremendous acceleration. Mrs. Johnson was a mother that other mothers would beg to spank their toddlers and talk sense to their teenagers and young adults. She was a powerful force in the Church and carried power tightly. She commanded a great influence, almost to the point of becoming a goddess to be feared and revered.

She was dark, short and thickset, with a face that gave no room for explanations. A first time encounter with her would remind you of a gun that is always ready for action.

The children never knew she had a soft side, until the day an incident happened. Thinking adults are infallible, immune to fear and could withstand whatever came their way, they were erroneously right until an experience shook them to the core of their being. It erased their young brains of the wrong assumptions.

Mr. Johnson had travelled on a business trip, leaving the four children to the mercy of their mother. They did their best to maintain, so as not to be punished. While going for women fellowship, Mrs. Johnson instructed them to cook and clean the house. This they did to the best of their abilities. They were packed on the settee, waiting for the arrival of Margaret Thatcher (that was what they called her behind her back), when the door opened in unceremoniously. Offence number one; they forgot to lock the door from inside. Kike pitied where the cane would land on her body. Tears were already welling in her always sorrowful eyes. She was the most fearful of the lot, being the only girl.

Surprisingly, their Mum was not bothered with the door she met ajar. Rather, she kept shaking like a chicken that fell into a basin of ice-cold water. Collapsing heavily into the settee, the voice that emanated from her did not sound like her voice. "Deacon Daniel is dead," she said.

Jeeeeeesuuuu! The news hit the children like thunderbolt. The Deacon Daniel they knew was a nice and God fearing man. He was at their house the day before, to pray against sudden death. Kike could still visualize him seated on the settee close to the TV set, his aging face surrounded by white spiky beards, his voice coming out gently in monotonous syllables. Kike's hair stood on end, and she instantly developed goose bumps. The thought in her 10-year-old mind was same with that of her other siblings. If death could enter Deacon Daniel's house and snatch him suddenly, what would be their lot?

Kike remembered the meat she stole from the pot of soup a day earlier. She remembered when Benjy lied to their Mum to evade beating. The children sat like chicks without the mother hen. They would have fared well under the wings of their Mum, but she was too cold for comfort.

When it was time to sleep, they rushed into the boys' room. Their thinking was that, the last person would be dragged back by the late Deacon's ghost. The boys had already promised to accommodate Kike for the night. Their house was a three bedroom flat which was constructed in a way that one room stood opposite the other two, with their large and well-spaced sitting room sitting majestically in between- like the owner of the house. Now in the room, the children heard their Mum's uncertain voice.

"Can you sleep alone?" she asked.

That was strange coming from her. She had never allowed any of them grow beyond a year in the parents' room. Thinking it was a ploy to give them a goodnight round of beating, as any answer that emanate from them could incite her, they answered carefully, "Yes ma! Thanks for asking."

But she wasn't done and asked again, "Are you sure you can sleep alone?"

Dutifully, they answered her, "Yes Mummy, thanks for asking."

Suddenly, it dawned on them that their Mum was also scared. Their militant mother was scared of Deacon Daniel's ghost. It sounded like Sunny Ade's music to their young ears. Like getting a long awaited Christmas gift. Mummy is scared! Mummy is scared! They danced to a silent song.

Maybe it was the devil that had been waiting all along to punish them that put a plan in their heads. They executed it without thinking of what the consequence would be. Standing by the window to their parents' room, Lekan- the eldest, repeatedly made funny sounds, with the intention to scare Mrs. Johnson.

Was she scared? She picked her Bible and started pleading the blood of Jesus. It was a funny sight, and the children enjoyed every bit of the drama. They went a step further by making Goke wrap himself in white, to stand at the entrance of their parents' unlocked room. The prank was made easier because there was power outage.

On sighting the supposed ghost, Mrs. Johnson dropped her Bible, sank to the floor and tried entering under the bed shouting, "Deacon Daniel, emi koni mopa e. I wasn't the one that killed you." It was the uncontrollable laughter from the children that made her realize her folly, and they got the beating of their lives that night.

THREE

If hell is on earth, Kike saw hell and entered. It was hot. It was fiery. She regretted the day she was born and the moment she took the decision to run after Jide Williams. She had ransacked her brain to look for a plausible reason to give for leaving the Church. Her Mum's in-depth scrutiny and harsh tones, couldn't allow her reason fast. So, she said whatever came to her mouth when questioned.

"Why did you leave the Bible study? Mrs. Johnson asked for the second time.

"At a time when the prayer meeting was about to start," Mr. Johnson added gently. "I saw you. I did."

"I…"Kike stammered.

"You what?"

"I met Martha, and Martha met me."

"What is she saying?" Her Mum irritably asked.

"I went to ease myself."

"Oh! You should have said that." Mrs. Johnson turned to her husband. "Deacon Johnson, your daughter took an hour to ease herself. She never came back till the service ended."

"It was because the toilet was dirty; I couldn't use it. Rather, I moved to the bush behind the Church to ease myself."

"I see," Mrs. Johnson said. She faced her husband again. "Daddy, you see what I always say? The Church toilet is not well maintained and monitored."

"Yes ma!" Kike cut in fearfully. "The last time I used it, I got toilet infection. That was why I decided to…"

"Shut up!" Mrs. Johnson shouted and landed Kike a slap that sent her rolling on the floor. "You mean it took you over an hour to ease yourself? Please tell me another story."

"I was coming to that," Kike said with hot tears cascading down her face. "After urinating, I was coming to the Church fast-fast, then I saw one of our choir members."

"So you stayed at the roadside to do choir rehearsal?" Mr. Johnson asked.

"No sir. I stayed to preach to him.

The parents were shocked at Kike's fallacious claims. "You should have left the preaching to the Pastor," Her mother mocked. "When did you become a preacher?"

"Actually, he wanted me to be his girlfriend."

"Hen?"

"So I told him that ha! It is not good."

"Okay."

"That God will not be happy with us, and my parents forbid such kind of relationship."

"So?"

"That was all. Then I was coming fast-fast, not knowing that I stayed long."

"You are a liar, a blatant liar." Her Mum pounced on her. Kicking her from all sides, she used all her appendages to pummel her and voiced out her disappointment. "You want to disgrace us? Knowing the kind of posts we hold in Church; knowing the kind of influence we command and how we challenge and discipline other peoples' children."

"You knew God from childhood," her father added, as he used his belt generously on her. "I will kill you before you shame us."

"I'm sorry Daddy," Kike pleaded.

"At no time did we draw back from taking you to Church. We adhered strictly to our denominational doctrines, religiously teaching you what is expected. You were part of the young star society, the girls' guild and now the young ladies guild. You are a strong member of the Sunday school team; a role model. Why will you disgrace us by spoiling your life?"

"I'm sorry Dad and Mum. I will never do it again."

"See! Ask your father," Mrs. Johnson boasted. "I came into his house with my hymen intact, and you must also marry as a virgin. I will do all in my power to ensure that. Abi, has someone ever slept with you?"

"No ma," Kike answered shaking her head.

Spent, they gave additional rules to further guide Kike's daily living. On no account should she be seen standing, sitting or talking with a man, either at the Church or elsewhere. She must never go out without being accompanied by either her elder brothers, or the younger one. Her skirts and gowns must henceforth reach up to her ankle.

Kike left for the room with her body drained of all strength. She felt her world falling apart, with nothing to hold it together. She wondered what her Mum's reaction would be, if she knew she was sexually active.

Kike was introduced to the adult game by a male classmate, a barrack boy that was too eager to satisfy her curiosity and answer her numerous questions about sex. It started gradually. She wanted to know if it was wrong to be attracted to the opposite sex, and why she always got funny feelings whenever she watched films involving sexually suggestive scene, or read one of the numerous novels she borrowed from her classmates. Innocently, she asked her Mother if getting attracted to boys or having funny feelings was wrong. She needed to know what to do about it.

Her Mum's reaction was discouraging. Shouting, she drew Kike to her room asking, "What did you know about sex? Mogbe! This girl wants to kill me. Oya, lie down." She forced her to lie down and checked if her hymen was intact. Heaving a sigh of relieve, she warned her never to mention the word sex in the house again.

"Why Mummy?" Kike asked.

"Because it is a dirty word," Her Mum replied.

If she had been given a chance, Kike might have asked if it was right to read romance novels and magazines, or watch the kind of movies her brothers often sneaked into the house when the parents were not around. Mrs. Johnson ordered her into the room, to prepare for a Bible competition that would hold by the next day. That ended the discussion between mother and daughter, although Kike's curiosity wasn't satisfied. She had increased sexual feelings day by day. And one day, she vented out to a likewise ignorant female classmate. Stanley the barrack boy eavesdropped on their discussion. He volunteered to teach Kike on all she needed to know. Persuading her to follow him to a friend's house, Stanley taught her that sex is beautiful and must be enjoyed even by teenagers. The first time with Stanley was painful, but she soon got used to him and then others, before Jide came her way.

'I'm in deep shit,' Kike murmured as she prepared for the night. What will happen if Mum gets to know that I missed my period? She searched her brain for what could have led to a missed period apart from pregnancy. God please help me, she prayed earnestly. If I scale through this, I will never go near a man again.

Possibly as a result of her prayer, or her menstrual blood that had been delayed for a week decided to use that moment to show up, or because of the beating she got, she felt something flow from her underneath. Kike looked down to see drops of blood splattering at her feet. Raising her night gown to confirm if the blood was from the right place, she twisted her waist in jubilation and relief.

After cleaning up and padding, she laid on the bed to sleep but sleep eluded her. Now that she has seen her menstrual flow, she feels a renewed tenderness towards Jide. Realizing that all her talk about reducing their sexual encounters was because of fear of the unknown, she wants him like never before.

Hugging her pillow, Kike stretched her hand to pick a novel she was reading before going to Church. Titled- The dark charming prince, it was about a man who tried all he could to get a maid to lay with him. Kike enjoyed the intrigues and the suspense and wished she was the maid being wooed by the hunk of a man. As she read and re-read about the sexual act that culminated from repeated attempts at seduction by the man, her senses became heightened, her sexual organs hyper-aroused, and she masturbated.

FOUR

Lord have your way in our midst today. In Jesus name I pray. The Choirmaster ended the opening prayer. Signaling everyone to stand up by raising his two palms, he instructed the keyboardist to start a prelude to get them set for a short praise session. The Church central choir was meeting in preparation for the revival service which would hold in a week time. It was a custom at Beulah Salvation Assembly to have a yearly revival, when a guest minister is invited to rekindle the fire of God in the life of the congregants.

Admonishing the Choristers, the Choirmaster said everyone should be prepared to minister wholeheartedly at the revival. He emphasized that since one cannot give what he lacks, it is important that all choristers check their lives, to make amendments wherever necessary, in order not to pollute the altar of God with strange fires. "Now to the business of the day" he said. "I want you to suggest and pick soul lifting and inspiring songs for rendition on every day of the revival."

There were diverse suggestions out of which he picked the songs he deemed suitable. Some of the Choristers were not okay with the choices and couldn't hide their feelings.

"The numbers picked are too slow," a female Chorister said. "To me, we should pick songs that are lively and danceable."

"I concur," another member said. "We shouldn't sing as if we are mourning. Remember the Bible says, in the presence of God, there is fullness of joy. We can only show our joy when we dance, shout and sing songs that are bubbly."

"Correct!" Kike stood up. "I want us to note that people

from different Churches will attend the program. It will be an opportunity to showcase our talents, and make people know that our choir is the best in town."

"I wonder if we are now in show business," someone whispered from the back.

"Anyway," the Choirmaster said with a raise of the hand to stop further input. "I want to correct a notion please. I have always drummed it into our ears that we sing not just to entertain, but to draw souls to the kingdom. If entertainment alone is what people need, they can get it from musicians that are not Christians. If we are only here to show our singing prowess, then we are not better than secular entertainers."

"Entertainment is part of the requirements to be a choir in vogue," Someone argued.

"It shouldn't be the main priority. Our focus should be how to use our songs to draw men to God. Any other thing is secondary and could be counterproductive."

All said and done, the songs were ratified and rehearsed over and over again. It was time to pick the worship leaders for the program. The Choirmaster turned to Jide Williams, the praise team coordinator. "Bro Jide," he called, what are your plans for the praise and worship sessions?"

"We will use a key worship leader, Miss Martha Aboderin, for the whole of the week," Jide answered. "She would be backed up by other praise team members."

Kike flinched and changed her facial expression the moment Jide made that statement. Not long after, she excused herself and stepped out. She also sent a message to Jide to meet her without delay.

"Why the distress call?" he asked on getting to her.

Kike refused to answer but eyed him and turned her face away.

"You better talk before the Choirmaster or someone meet us here."

"Why should Martha lead the worship for the whole of the revival week? Why not me or someone else? She fumed.

"Why not her?"

"Everything is Martha! Martha! Martha this, Martha that. I doubt if you are not dating her. I caught the two of you making faces at each other today."

"Is that all?" Jide asked, trying hard to conceal his anger. "I need to go back inside."

"Won't you say anything?" she held him by the cloth.

"What did you want me to say? This lady is your friend. The decision for her to lead was unanimously taken based on her ability. Now that you say I'm dating her, maybe I should begin to think towards that direction."

"I'm sorry."

"Let's go in before people start thinking otherwise."

"It's okay! When do we meet again?"

"It depends on you." Jide replied impatiently. Next week is fine."

"No!" she frowned. "Next week is revival week."

"The ball is in your court." He left her standing.

After the rehearsal ended, Martha waited at the gate for Jide to join her. Holding hands, they took a back street leading to Martha's home.

"What were you discussing with Kike," She asked.

"Hun?"

"Don't feign ignorance. I saw you discussing with her."

"That girl is a nuisance," Jide replied and drew her close.

"I'm beginning to suspect the two of you." Martha turned her back to him. "I caught you making faces at each other at the rehearsal today."

"Look Martha." He turned her to face him. "I can't stoop so low, as to have anything to do with that girl. She's lousy, she's uncultured and she's not even beautiful. You know you are my one and only. Although, you are not treating me well. I'm a virile young man with flesh and blood, and your continuous insistence on no sex before marriage is demoralizing."

"So?"

"You shouldn't expect me not to have it with other girls. Body no be wood. But Kike is below my standard. I got nothing to do with her."

"If you say so."

"On a serious note Martha, this no sex thing is killing me."

"How? Our agreement at the start of this relationship was that, we would save physical sex till our wedding night. But, I do everything to satisfy you. We kiss, smooch, rub and do it from the back. Besides, we engage in phone sex and you have my nudes. What else do you want? I even…"

"Even what? Say it! Jide prompted, raising up her chin. "Are you shy to say it?"

"Must I say everything?" she leaned against a wall.

"Don't think I'm not appreciative of all we do together," Jide said. "The little you show me now, gives me the confidence that you will be good in the other room. You know, I have this notion that God made your mouth to give utmost satisfaction. No one would believe the mouth you use to sing and inspire people at Church, is the same mouth you use to give me joy at the right place. Honestly, you are good at what you do."

"I don't like it," Martha objected and rose to her full height. "That is touching and far below the belt. When I hear you talk at times, I remember touts at the park. Must you say everything? No one that hears you making such reckless utterance will believe that you are a Christian."

"You may say whatever you want to say about me Martha," he replied. The truth is that my Christian life and my societal life is different. My activities in the Church cannot stop me from enjoying life. I'm a young man, who does not want to grow up regretting not living his life to the fullest."

"And you are free to live your life to the fullest," Martha sarcastically said. Because, no one would ask you for the proof of your virginity when you get married. The woman is always at the receiving end. You know what? I'm under obligation that my hubby must present a blood stained cloth as a proof of my chastity to my parents after my first wedding night. I must keep myself so that I could boldly say to the Pastor during the wedding counselling, that I am a virgin. So, be satisfied with what you get. Don't ask me for sex again. But, I will do all that is needed to be done in order to keep a man; that wouldn't do the actual thing until the D-day. Good night."

"Fire cracker," Jide whispered. He whistled, rubbed his head, drew his goatee and gave a wicked laugh. Considering his experience with other girls, he knew it was matter of time before Martha would fall under his amorous advances like a pack of cards. 'They are all the same,' he murmured. 'Church girl or no Church girl.' Dragging his six-foot frame and well-built body that made him irresistible to all category of ladies as he always claimed, he picked a stone and threw it into the compound next to Martha's'. That was the sign needed for his next meat to come out. That meat was already on the slab and will be slaughtered today. At the back of her compound. The night was still young.

FIVE

The long awaited revival started as scheduled. The revivalist was an elderly and vibrant minister who gave the word of God in its raw form, not minding whose ox was gored. His Bible exposition was done in such a way that, it would leave one with no doubt that he had the backing of God.

Like Paul, he said he was an anti-Christ before his conversion. God had mercy on him and saved him. Therefore, he was eager for all to have genuine salvation through an encounter with the Savior. He emphasized on the need for Christians to work out their salvation with fear and trembling (Philippians 2: 12) because, now is their salvation nearer than when they first believed (Romans 13:11).

Furthermore, he reiterated that many had gone the broad way because of the cares and entanglements of the world. Darkness had crept steadily into the Church, making peoples' lamps dim and ineffective. He enjoined everyone to take the narrow way that leads to paradise.

According to him, it's not in vogue to see preachers preaching about salvation. Majority of altar calls don't produce needed fruits. That is why the Church is filled with workers who are not walkers with God. Many are busy laboring for God without knowing him. There are Sunday school teachers who do not live by what they teach. Choristers that are singing to hell. Ushers who commit wilful sins. Preachers that embezzle Church money. The Church is full of strive, envy and rancor. Instead of being a place where sinners will see light and embrace it, it is fast becoming a dumping ground for unrepentant sinners. The Church has entered into the world and the world into the Church. Emphasizing on

Galatians 5:19-21, he said, the works of the flesh is manifesting among brethren, who mustn't forget that Christ will come for a Church that is holy and without blemish (Ephesians 5: 27).

"But!" he bellowed on the last day of the revival, "The Lord knows those who are his, and everyone calling on the name of the Lord should depart from evil!" After that, he led the congregation in singing the hymn-

Have you been to Jesus for the cleansing power?

Are you washed in the blood of the lamb?

Are you fully trusting in his Grace this hour?

Are you washed in the blood of the lamb?

The refrain was taken loud and strong

Are you washed in the blood?

In the soul cleansing blood of the lamb?

Are your garments spotless?

Are they white as snow?

Are you washed in the blood of the lamb?

Martha was pricked to the depth of her heart, as she listened to the preacher. Feeling a deep sense of anguish and dread for her life, she shook at the thought of what would happen if she refused to give her life to Christ. Although she had answered to an altar call at a time she needed to be baptized to become a full member of the Church, her secret life style was such that wouldn't make Christ happy.

To the society, she was a decent and well behaved girl. To the Church, she was dedicated, God-fearing and a role model. To her parents, she was a child they trusted and will always be proud of. It was only Martha that knew the secret sins she contended with. The sins that easily beset her and made her vulnerable to other sins. She knew her heart wasn't right with God, and she feared what would happen if the trumpet should sound. When the preacher gave an altar call for all that would give their lives to Christ to step forward, she made a move which coincided with him asking the choir to lead - I surrender all.

Martha wanted to be at the front, at the altar to plead for mercy, not minding what people would say. As the choirmaster shoved the mic into her hand, she closed her eyes, knelt at the spot, and sang the song from deep within her. She felt a great burden leave her and an indescribable joy suffuse her. Tears ran down her face as she made the decision to follow Christ to the end.

When she got home and all had retired for the night except her Mum who needed to put things together for the next morning, Martha joined her in the kitchen and explained what happened to her.

"Mum, I rededicated my life to Christ today at the service," she started.

"Who was ruling your life before, the devil?" her mother raised an eyebrow.

"Not really. I was touched by the preaching of the revivalist," Martha answered. "It made me realize that my life was not totally right with God."

"Interesting."

"I was about answering the altar call when the revivalist asked the choir to sing. Well, right at the spot where I stood, I rededicated my life to Christ with a covenant to shun every sin and be a child of God."

"Thank God you didn't get a chance to move to the altar."

"What's bad about it?"

"I swear, I would have skinned you with my bare hands."

"I'm confused and don't understand you. What is bad about answering an altar call? Is that not the essence of Christianity? To decide for Christ."

"Definitely you are confused," her Mum answered. You were emotionally carried away by the sweet mouth of the preacher. Remember people hold you in high esteem and see you as a role model for the youths. It would be shameful for them to know you've not given your life to Christ as you claimed. What is there to give?"

"Mummy!"

"You were born into a Christian home. To practicing Christian parents, dedicated to the service of God. You've been engaged in one form of service or the other from childhood. I ask again, what are you giving? Daughter, your life is perfect the way it is."

"I still feel…"

"Don't feel anything because, tomorrow is another day. Have a nice night rest and make sure you read psalm 91. Keep the Bible under your pillow before you sleep."

Dismissed, Martha left for her room in a dejected mood, feeling like a deflated balloon. She sat and brooded, wondering why her Mum of all people would be skeptical about her public declaration of Christ. What is the essence of attending Church if not to get saved? She asked. Why would one pretend to be what he's not in order to look good before people?

She queried if her parents' salvation was genuine? With what she heard at the Church, she doubted their salvation, and she concluded that it might be difficult for them to admit that they are not saved, except by divine intervention. Thinking about some questionable characters in them despite being strongholds in the Church; characters like lying, cheating and slandering, characters like pride and envy, Martha shook her head.

Her Dad would force the children to lie for him. He deliberately falsified her younger brother's age because, he wanted him to write the National common entrance at age 8. He also hired someone to write Mathematics and Physics for her elder brother in his external GCE. He had written several times without success.

Her Mum would lie and call it a white lie. She would gossip and slander, without batting an eye lid. She would manipulate to get positions in the Church. She's never tired of pitting people against one another to achieve her selfish aims.

Her parents were full of religious activities like the Pharisees. They were like tombs that looked beautiful outside, but contained dead bones inside. They were blind teachers of the blind. Martha detested their kind of Christianity. She wanted a life that is upright and devoid of hypocrisy. She wanted a life that would portray Christ and lead others to him. Kneeling by her bedside, she prayed for God to give her the Grace to stand firm and not be distracted.

SIX

On a warm Saturday evening, Martha arrived at the Church for the choir rehearsal in preparation for the yearly carol service. She was dressed in a flowery patterned yellow gown which ran down to a little below her knee. Running late, she hurried without noticing two middle aged women -Mrs. Johnson and Mrs. Williams, who were on a bench close to the Church entrance. They sat close, talking and whispering to each other. They were keen on everyone entering the Church, especially the youths. They were like school prefects waiting to catch late comers. They watched, they commented and sneered. They called Martha, she turned and curtsied.

"Eku irole ma," she said.

"I thought we are two small for you to greet," Mrs. Johnson replied.

"I'm sorry," she pleaded. I'm in a hurry to get to the choir practice."

"That's okay," Mrs. Williams said and asked after her parents.

"They are fine ma."

Moving close to her, Mrs. Johnson held her cloth at the neckline and tried pulling it up. "This neckline is too low, it's almost showing your breast."

"Mummy!" Martha frowned and removed her hand. "That's the reason why I have an inner wear under."

"Must you wear this kind of cloth? It's too showy," Mrs. Johnson insisted. "See the flowers on it. And your head is not properly covered. A child of God must be dressed appropriately, with no strand of hair showing. Look at your gown. Don't you see that it's too short?

"It's below the knee, Martha replied."

"Didn't your mother see you before you left the house? Mrs. Johnson asked. "I trust my daughter Kike. She will never dress like this."

Martha refused replying but checked her wrist watch.

"You are even checking your watch," Mrs. Johnson continued, telling me that I'm wasting your time?"

"No ma. It's just that I don't agree that my dressing is out of place."

"I tell you that this dress is not modest. I have the mind to send you back home, and as a Deaconess of this Church I have the right to do so. For God's sake, I will allow you to go in for what you came for. But next time," Mrs. Johnson emphasized by pulling her right ear. "Remember! Your gown must be down to your ankle, your hair must be properly covered, and your earring must not dangle."

"I wonder if those are new laws," Martha grumbled. She was almost at a point of shedding tears.

"You have guts," Mrs. Williams exclaimed. "Is that how you talk to your Mother at home?"

"I'm sorry ma." Martha looked sideways.

"With this kind of character, there's no way you won't pollute well trained children in the Church."

"With due respect ma, I am a saved child of God."

"Meaning?"

"I can't pollute anyone because I'm not polluted. I don't know why you are always picking on me."

"Jesus!" Mrs. Johnson screamed. "You've over stepped your

boundary. Now! Go back home," she pointed towards the gate. "Go and tell your mother that I disallowed you from entering the Church. Let her give you the home training you lack."

"I wish you will be more concerned with the spiritual life of the people in the Church and not just their outward appearance," Martha said. "God knows you are picking on me unjustly because my dressing is as good as anybody's." Martha was in tears as she left the Church compound.

Turning to each other, the two Deaconesses gave a knowing smile as Mrs. Williams mouthed, "What audacity?"

"Leave her. She's growing wings," Mrs. Johnson replied. "It is because everyone is calling her good girl, as if our own children are not good. She is always at the fore front of every one of them."

"That will soon stop."

"What do you mean?" Mrs. Johnson moved closer to her.

"Didn't you notice something?"

"Like what?"

"Are you not a woman?"

"Meaning?"

Mrs. Williams whispered into her left ear. "She's pregnant."

"Oti o! It's not possible. Pregnant?" Mrs. Johnson shouted.

"I can detect a day old pregnancy in a matured woman, talk less of a girl that is 3 months gone."

"Tell me another story," Mrs. Johnson eagerly said.

"Didn't you see that her breasts are bigger, and her waistline is thicker?"

Mrs. Johnson retied her wrapper and clapped her hands before speaking again. Scornfully, she said, "and she wants to continue climbing the altar to defile it. The Pastor must hear this." Hastening towards the Pastor's office, her friend trailed after her, with her arthritic knees making her to lag behind.

"Where are you going?" she panted.

"To intimate the Pastor."

"We have not verified."

"Are you not sure of what you saw?"

"Doubly sure."

"Wonders shall never end." They rushed to the Pastor, beaming as if they had the most important news of the year.

Revd. Bamiro was dumbfounded when he heard what they had to say. "Are you sure? Has she been tested?" He asked. "The Bible says we should find out all things, and hold on to the truth."

"I'm very sure of what I saw Sir," Mrs. Williams responded. "I can recognize a day old pregnancy in a snail, talk less of a fully grown lady."

"Let's put the snail part aside," the Pastor said, sinking into a chair. "If it turns out to be true, it would be very bad."

"On the contrary sir, it is good that we are able to discover in time before she does something funny to it." Mrs. Johnson chipped in.

"Isn't it bad that our children are going wayward and doing contrary to what we taught them from the cradle?" the Pastor emphasized.

"Hmmm."

"Is it the problem of the Church? Or negligence from the parents? Where are we getting it wrong? I'm pricked to the heart," he lamented.

"We should continue to discipline them, for others to learn when witness their disgrace and humiliation," Mrs. Johnson suggested.

"It's not working. We've had to discipline four members in the space of a year. Immorality is rife in the Church despite all the teachings we give," The Pastor cried.

"In my opinion," Mrs. Johnson said, "the punishment being meted out is mild. That's why our kids continue sleeping around. Then, the parents too are to be blamed. I don't see how a girl will be under my roof and be sleeping with a man up to the extent of getting pregnant for months and I will not know. It's bad and the parents as well should face the music."

"You have a point there madam," the Pastor said and asked, "What do we do about the case?"

"We have to confront her."

"Let her tell us what happened and the person responsible."

"Fine. Nevertheless, we should take it easy and thread softly," the Pastor cautioned. "So that we don't accuse her wrongly. I still have some misgivings about the issue. That girl is decent, and I have a witness in me that she's a child of God."

"Okay o."

"Don't get me wrong. I'm not trying to defend whatever she might have done. If she's really pregnant, she would face the wrath of the Church."

"Yes sir!"

"The Church is delegating the two of you to do a thorough investigation. If possible, go to her parent, interview the girl, and come back with facts. I give you two days to get back to me."

"Yes sir," Mrs. Johnson answered.

SEVEN

The carnal mind is deceitful, wicked and has no capacity for the kind of love that God extended towards man by sending his son to die as propitiation for sin. The religious humans without God's kind of love do not have the mind of Christ and would do anything to pull others down. They cast stones. They rejoice at the downfall of others. They are extremely judgmental.

Leaving the Pastor's office, the two Deaconesses made straight for the home of the Aboderins', planning on how to throw dirt on the face of the bank- executive wife and the Professor husband. To them, they always behaved as if they were the only blessed people in the Church.

Mrs. Aboderin was not keen on letting them in, especially for what they did to her daughter. "Why have you both constituted yourselves as Sanballats in the Church?" she asked. She pointed at them and shook her head. "Why are you always poke nosing into the affairs of others? Always looking for faults and casting stones."

"Mrs. Aboderin," Mrs. Williams called gently. We don't know what your daughter came home to tell you. We were only trying to be good Christians by correcting her."

"By telling her she's not well trained? Mrs. Aboderin asked. "Common! Remember the Church is for all of us."

"Madam please we are sorry if what we did offended you," Mrs. Johnson responded sharply while holding her hands up. "I beg you to sit and listen to what we came to tell you. We have a bigger problem in our hands."

"What problem that we can't discuss at Church tomorrow?"

"The Pastor sent us here."

The word 'Pastor' was what calmed Mrs. Aboderin and made her allow them into the house. Leading them to a seat, she sank into another and demanded for the message.

Mrs. Johnson cleared her throat and shifted forward. She said. "This is a kind of message one will not be happy to relay. But how do I refuse the work of God?"

Mrs. Aboderin's adrenaline shot up at the words of the Deaconess. She wondered what could have happened that would warrant the Pastor sending them to her. Her mind drifted to her husband on sabbatical in another state. If something had happened to him, definitely it wouldn't be these holier than thou personalities that would be sent to her. And her children? All were safely at home except the one on campus.

"Has anything happened to my husband or my boy at the University? She fearfully asked.

"No madam, on the contrary we came concerning Martha."

"Yes! What about Martha? Why can't you leave her alone? Even the Reverend?"

"Please calm down ma," Mrs. Williams pleaded. "It is a serious issue."

"I'm all ears," Martha's Mum responded, adjusting on the seat.

The two women looked at each other to know who would bell the cat. They both turned to face Mrs. Aboderin and looked at her for so long that she got embarrassed and averted her face. Clearing her throat, Mrs. Johnson asked if Mrs. Aboderin had noticed any change in Martha.

"Change?"

"Like weight gain, increased sleeping, tiredness, signs and symptoms of..."

"Symptoms of what?" she flared up. "What audacity? You

are evil minded."

"Who is evil minded?" Mrs. Johnson responded with equal heat. "Bring out your daughter. Let's clear the air. Some people noticed strange things about her, and the Pastor instructed us to come and find out. Is there any harm in that?

"What happens if your insinuation is wrong?

"That will be between you and the Pastor. We are doing our job as sent."

Mrs. Aboderin stood up to go in and call her daughter, but the women stopped her.

"There's no need to go inside. Shout for her."

She felt invaded and intimidated and wanted to send the two away. She knew she needed to maintain her cool. She would rather call Martha and shame them.

Martha was called. Oblivious to what had transpired, she thought the women were there to give a report on what happened at the Church.

"Madam! Look very well," Mrs. Williams pointed. "Are there no visible changes in your daughter?"

"Oh! Now I understand," Mrs. Aboderin responded. "If it is about her weight gain, it's because she just finished WAEC. She has been staying home and resting a lot. What else do you want to know?'

"Please ask her of the last time she menstruated," Mrs. Williams demanded.

Mrs. Aboderin had started feeling funny and uneasy. The kind of feeling you have when it looks as if your adversary has an information that could give him an edge over you. It was glaring that Martha had added much weight, with her feminine features looking ballooned. She had been complaining of nausea and loss of appetite for close to a month, and often looked tired and worn out after little work. "Oh! This is not happening," Mrs. Aboderin whispered. Sweat broke out on her forehead as she held firmly to the arms of the chair. Fearfully she said, "Martha look at me, when was the last time you menstruated?"

"Menstruation?" Martha asked in an uncertain voice.

"Yes! Menstruation! Blood! Her mother screamed.

"Three months. I think three months," she answered, raising three fingers.

"What? This girl has killed me," her Mum screamed again.

"Mum, you know my period has never been regular," Martha explained. "It comes every three month."

"Thank God." She clamped her palms together. "Can you people see? She said while stretching her hands towards the two Deaconesses. "I'm sure it will come very soon."

"Indeed!" Mrs. Williams winced. "I still have a question to ask her."

"What else do you want? She has given you an explanation for her missed period. What else do you want?"

"Madam. The changes in your daughter depicts nothing but pregnancy."

"Martha," Mrs. Johnson cut in, "I have another question. I want you to answer me truthfully."

"Okay ma."

"Look at me straight in the face."

"Yes ma."

"Have you been with a man?"

"Been with a man?"

"You know what I mean. Did you sleep with a man?"

Martha turned to her mother; who was eagerly waiting for a negative response and burst into tears saying, "Mummy! I was forced. I was raped."

Mrs. Aboderin fainted.

EIGHT

It took lots of courage for Martha to present herself at the Church on the day the penalty for her derailment was announced. Not with the fact that she had become a pariah to everyone, including her parents and siblings. No one believed that the act that led to her pregnancy was a forced one as she claimed.

Immediately the Deaconesses left the Aboderins' on the day of the confrontation, they moved back to the Pastorium, not minding that it was late into the night. Expressing their disappointments as they gave the Pastor the feedback, they advised that action should be taken swiftly before the pregnancy could be harmed.

Martha was tested and confirmed to be three months gone. Her parents were devastated and nearly died from shame and heartbreak. Her Dad had to be summoned back from his station to stand by his wife, who was almost having a mental breakdown.

Even before the Pastor made an official announcement, majority of the Church members were in the know. They warned their children to beware of the Aboderins because, the children were wayward. Before then, the Church council had invited Martha into their midst for further verification and counselling, preparatory to disciplinary action.

At the meeting with the council, Martha sat in between her parents; both of whom were bowed and shrunken from shame especially because of several accusatory eyes looking at them. Albeit, there were some kind and sympathetic faces among the council members, but such were few, very few. Both parents tried as much as possible to sit far away from Martha. One was to the wall and the other to the end of the bench as if they were dissociating from her. She had not trusted them enough to mention the name of the person responsible for her predicament. She insisted she would only talk when she got to the council meeting. They sat facing the council members who were on chairs around a mahogany table, with the Pastor at the head.

Without mincing words, Revd. Bamiro confirmed what almost everyone knew; that Martha Aboderin was carrying a three months old pregnancy, as confirmed at the laboratory and through scanning. He condemned what had happened in its entirety and emphasized that stiff penalty would be taken against her and whosoever was responsible for the pregnancy, if he happened to be a member of the Church. Nevertheless, he admonished everyone to look at the happening from the perspective of love and have the mind to encourage and be kind to the Aboderins, at such a trying period. He said since Christ came for all and sundry including those that are presumed sinners, no one should be condemned but rather, Christians should carry one another's burden in love. After that, the questioning began.

For how long has Martha been sexually active? She answered that she was a virgin, and the event that led to the pregnancy was her first sexual experience. Asked if she had ever noticed some characters to show that her daughter had been seeing men, Mrs. Aboderin took the boldness to stare directly at the council members, replying that nothing had ever been suggestive of such. Martha had always been a decent girl, and she was yet to come to term on what had befallen her. She was further asked if Martha had mentioned the name of the person that put her in the family way. On hearing that, Mrs. Aboderin burst into tears. She said, "That is the problem. Despite the beating, the cajoling and everything, she refused to talk. She insisted that she will only mention the name at the Church council."

"Ngbo Martha? The Pastor asked, "Who is responsible for your pregnancy?"

Martha looked up and said, "I waited to mention the name here because, if I do so before now, he might look for a way to extricate himself. He warned that on no account should I tell anyone about what happened. I threatened to tell my Mum the day I was raped, but he said no one would believe me. And really, I made a great mistake by honoring the invitation to his house, knowing he had been pestering me for sex."

"Story- story," Mrs. Johnson whispered into Mrs. Williams's ear.

"Wait Martha," the Pastor cut her short. "You will have all the time to tell us about what happened. Who is the man that raped you?"

Martha looked at the Pastor, her parents, the council members, then pointed to the door saying, "He's out there in the choir. He's having choir practice with them and I can't even join."

"What? Who?" the Pastor asked gently.

"Looking towards the two Deaconesses at the back, Martha emphatically called the name- Jide.

"Jide," the Pastor repeated.

"Yes! Jide Williams. The coordinator of the praise team."

"It is not possible," Mrs. Williams bellowed. She dashed towards Martha as if she would pounce on her. "You can't rope my son into your mess, just because I was the one that first discovered that you were pregnant, before you could abort it as usual. What a liar? What a useless girl?"

"I beg your pardon," Mrs. Aboderin charged up. "My daughter is not useless."

"Then she should stop trying to implicate innocent people. What will my son do with this thing? He's a graduate awaiting youth service. A well brought up son."

"It doesn't count," an elder spoke from behind. "You can't just trust the children of this age."

"The girl is not sure of what she's saying," another elder said.

The room became rowdy as the council members exchanged words. It took lots of effort before the Pastor could restore order. Facing Martha, he asked if she was sure of the accusation.

"I'm very sure sir," she responded. "He forced me and slept with me."

"When?"

"A week after the revival service. Precisely on August 25."

"Where?"

"In his parents' sitting room."

"This is a tricky knot that needs to be loosened carefully," the Pastor said. "Our aim as a Church is to do justice to all and let no offender go scot free. Deaconess Williams," he called. "Where were you on August 25?"

"I wasn't in town," Mrs. Williams responded. "I and Daddy were at a wedding in Kano. Pastor, this girl is lying. My son can never do such."

"Don't worry. We will get to the root of it," the Pastor responded. He sent for Jide.

Jide expressed utmost surprise as he entered the room to behold the faces of the council members, consisting of Church elders and Deacons.

After responding to his greeting, the Pastor apologized for calling him out of the choir and threw the first question at him. "Son," he said. "Look at the lady seated there." He pointed to Martha. "Did you know her?"

"Yes sir," Jide smiled. "She's Martha Aboderin, one of our choristers."

"What else did you know about her?"

"Nothing more than she's a praise leader in the Church,

and..."

"And what?"

"I don't know if it is appropriate to say it here."

"You are free to say anything," the Pastor responded.

NINE

Jide was a smooth talker and an engager. He also possessed a charm that kept both the young and old mesmerized whenever he spoke. Even before he was invited, a good number of the council members already had the notion that he couldn't have raped Martha as she claimed; except if the whole world was going crazy. Jide had always portrayed himself as a true child of God, both in manner and speech. So, what would make him commit an abominable act of raping a choir member?

He had always claimed that he could have any girl in the Church. He had evidences of missives from several ladies who wanted him at all cost. His skillfulness on almost every musical instrument, his talent of singing in addition to his natural charm, personality and look, made everyone want to associate with him. Some even claimed God showed him to them as their future partner. Jide would claim he's patiently waiting for his bone of bone and flesh of flesh.

To what he felt reluctant in saying to the council members, he cleared his throat, looked around and maintained focus, as if he was canvassing for support. He said, "For some time now, Martha has been running after me, telling me she loves me. At first I thought it is just a crush. But, I became alarmed when she begged me to sleep with her. She promised to give me utmost satisfaction because she's experienced."

"What? No! Prof Aboderin shouted. "This show of shame is too much. I can't bear it. I'm out of here."

"Prof. please don't leave," the Pastor pleaded.

"I shouldn't leave?" Professor Aboderin asked. "With all I've heard? I can't believe my daughter is the one he's talking about. Young man, are you being truthful to us?"

"Of course," Jide replied confidently. "I warned her off sternly with a threat to report to her mother, if she doesn't desist from pestering me." He produced a phone from his pocket and pointed it at the Prof. "I have evidences here," he said. "I had been deleting several. I kept only two because of a day like this. I have always believed a day like this would come."

Revd. Bamiro collected the phone quickly because, he wasn't sure of the kind of evidence Jide would produce. He felt the Prof. could have a heart attack if he got another shocker. Jide moved near to him, scrolled to a media content and opened. The pastor shouted 'Jesus' and averted his face.

"That is one of the nudes she sent to me, when I refused to accept her advances," Jide claimed.

"No! No! No!" the Pastor repeatedly said, shaking his head."

"Pass it round and let us see the image of shame," Mrs. Johnson requested.

"No," the Pastor said and restrained Jide. He faced Martha. "Young lady, what do you have to say?" he asked.

"Sir! That picture was sent with mutual consent," she answered. "We were in a relationship for a year. He always request that I send my nudes to him."

"That is not the only evidence that I have," Jide interrupted. "There are also series of text messages, where she begged me to go down with her."

"Hun?"

"Sir, look at this." Jide passed the phone to the Pastor again. Revd. Bamiro collected the phone and read out a text.

I had a dream yesterday. You were all over me: kissing, smooching and giving me from the back. I can't wait to have you.

"Jeeeeeeesuuuuuuuu!" Mrs. Johnson shouted."

"Eyi o dara. This is not good," the Pastor lamented.

"He's lying," Martha cried. "We were dating."

"You said you were a virgin before the rape. What about the naked picture and the kissing text? Ha!"

"It was a mutual thing Sir."

"Shut up!" Mrs. Johnson shouted. "You have guts. Let's call a spade a spade. This is what you get when parents don't give quality time to child training." She intentionally eyed Mrs. Aboderin. "Today you are in Sokoto. Tomorrow you are in Kafanchan. Next tomorrow you are in Lagos, looking for money, fame and career progression. You don't even know about the happenings in your child's life. It is a big shame. This girl is not fit to be in the midst of well-trained children like ours.

"And she's looking for who to implicate," Mrs. Williams chipped in.

"I'm not implicating anyone. Jide was my boyfriend," Martha insisted.

"Okay. Did you have any of his messages on your phone? Like the one you sent to him."

"No sir," Martha replied. "He always insisted, that I delete his messages. He said I might be careless, and my parents would get to know about us."

Martha cried like her heart would break. On the other hand, Jide had a confident look, knowing he had carried the day.

"He's lying," Martha insisted. "We dated for close to a year. I made a crucial decision at the last revival which warranted me quitting the relationship. I intimated him. He begged that I meet him at home to have further discussions, since his parents won't be around. I went to him, and he raped me. I was a virgin until he raped me."

Martha's deep sobbing touched the heart of few of the council members, who thought there must be some truths to her narration, but Jide insisted on his story. Turning to Martha the Pastor said, "You said you were with him on…"

"August 25," she insisted.

"Can you say the actual time you were together?"

"3pm sir."

"Are you sure?" the Pastor asked.

Martha thought hard before replying, "I think 3pm."

"Jide, where were you by 3pm on that day?" the Pastor inquired.

Jide smiled before replying. "Sir, I was with you at the Pastorium at that time on the said day. You can testify to it. After our meeting, I stayed back to practice on the keyboard. I never left the Church until the choir rehearsal began and ended. The sexton saw me when I was practicing, and I even sent him to get kosai and dankali."

"Martha," the Pastor called. "Jide was actually with me at the said time on the said day. Although, I can't vouch for his movement beyond 3:30."

"Maybe I missed the time. I'm somewhat confused," Martha cried.

"Do you have a witness, someone that saw you going to him, or someone you told before going?"

The whole council held their breath. Martha hesitated. "I did not tell anyone," she responded. "The relationship was a closely guided secret."

"You mean no one saw you?"

"Yes, except…"

"Except who?" the Pastor asked wearily.

"As I tried opening the gate into their compound, it was pushed from within and Kike Johnson stepped out."

"My daughter?" Mrs. Johnson exclaimed. "You can't be serious. She was at a coaching center at the said day and time."

"Deaconess please calm down and let her talk," the Pastor pleaded.

"We were both surprised to see each other," Martha continued. She claimed her mother sent her to drop a parcel for Deaconess Williams but met her absence. I in turn told her I wanted to collect the Sunday school manual from Jide. She said she was rushing to the coaching center for JAMB lesson."

The Pastor sent for Kike, who denied vehemently that she was anywhere near the Williams' residence on the said day. Facing Martha she said, "You want to drag me into your problem. Haven't I warned you to stop sleeping around? Why did you want to implicate me?"

"Kike! We greeted on that day. You were in a blue gown with yellow patterns."

"That you saw when we met at the Church. My Mum can testify that the driver dropped me at the coaching center and picked me to Church after lesson hours. I can call the driver as a witness. We had biology on the said day. I can call my mates to vouch that I was at the coaching center throughout. I never left for a single minute."

"That's okay Kike," the Pastor said. "There might be no need for further witnesses as we have seen where the matter is heading to. I want us to give time to pray and ask the Holy Spirit for guidance. There are dark clouds around this issue. We are not too sure of what to hold as the truth."

Majority of the council members objected to the Pastor's suggestion, emphasizing that the truth had been revealed. To them, Martha was trying to implicate the others, especially with the inconsistencies in her story. Furthermore, they threatened to boycott any other meeting if the right thing was not done because, it looked as if the Pastor was trying to cover and acquit

Martha. They said the Holy Spirit had revealed all that needed to be revealed in the meeting, and nothing contrary coming from the Pastor would be accepted.

TEN

The pronouncement was swift and precise. Everyone held their breath to know what would be done to sinner-girl that had all along been pretending to be a Christian. The Pastor climbed the pulpit, fixed his glasses atop the bridge of his nose, cleared his throat and began. He instructed Martha to stand and face the congregation. Looking straight at the people, he said, "Martha acted against the will of God by engaging in premarital sex that resulted in an unwanted pregnancy, to which she couldn't pinpoint a single person that impregnated her. She lied to the Church and tried implicating innocent people. Therefore, she is suspended from being a Church worker. She will have a special seat at the front of the congregation, where she must always be at every service."

Martha couldn't raise her head, to behold the people who had always listened to her sing and hear her teach. She was dressed in a black garb, like someone in mourning. Her 4-feet- plus frame looked diminished. Right there at the front of the Church, she looked vulnerable, with no support system at all.

The women were the most affected with the pronouncement, and they expressed their emotions in diverse ways. Some cried, some nodded in support of the penalty, while some felt unconcerned. A particular girl in the choir was ecstatic, since Martha would stop being a hindrance to her showcasing her talent.

The Pastor continued by calling on Prof. & Mrs. Aboderin to be on their feet. It was only the wife that was present because, Martha's father had refused to be a party to the show of shame. Traveling back to his station the day after the council meeting, he told his family not to expect him in a long time.

"After deliberating on what your daughter did," the pastor announced, "and your complicity in not exposing her in good time. The Church council has decided to remove you from all leadership positions for a period of one year. We pray God will grant you the Grace to make amendments where necessary."

After that, the Pastor turned to the congregation and said, "We want to put a mechanism in place to check mate our young men and women from engaging in premarital sex. We discovered that, even with the teachings and admonitions, our youngsters still go behind to do whatever they like. Therefore, there will be an active monitoring system from now on." He paused, then continued by saying, "I humbly call on Deaconess Johnson to come forward." Mrs. Johnson moved to the front with head held high.

"You are going to help our boys and girls to maintain a firm stand against fornication."

"Yes sir."

"You will checkmate, teach and monitor their activities, with the Church giving you the necessary support and encouragement."

"Thank you sir."

"And now," the Pastor continued. "I stand as a minister of God, to ask all our young people that are virgins to come to the altar. Remember you are in the presence of God," the Pastor warned. "We want only virgins. Those that are not virgins will fit into another program that we are presently working on."

There was slight hesitation from the audience. Then as if on cue, the young people began trooping to the front, especially the ladies. Tall, short, dark, fair, slim and plump, almost all the unmarried people stood up. Mrs. Johnson scanned to see if Kike was among them. She smiled on sighting her. She whispered, I trust my daughter.

The Pastor looked at all that came out and reduced his eye

to a slit. "Well," he said hesitatingly. "If you all say you are virgins, then we will take you as virgins. I hand you over to God and Deaconess Johnson. She's a tested and trusted mother, and will help in guiding you to the right path. Remember, you are brides of Jesus and mustn't get defiled. Christ will come for a bride without blemish." The Church applauded as the service came to a close, with the declaration of Grace by the Pastor.

The homeward journey for the Johnsons was quiet. Everyone was engrossed in different thoughts. Mrs. Johnson tried engaging the others in conversation because she was in a good mood. She was basking in the euphoria of the honor received at the Church. Her husband concentrated on driving, while the children looked as if they were terrified. Mrs. Johnson had expected them to gist all the way home, especially on the trending topic of Martha's punishment. But they behaved as if they were mourning someone dear to them.

Kike looked pale. Beads of sweat broke out on her forehead. She refused to look at anyone, but insisted she wanted fresh air and placed herself close to the window. It was in the process of opening the door to the house that a wave of dizzy spell overtook her, and she went down.

ELEVEN

The atmosphere at Crystal Medical center was tense. Kike's agitated parents paced from one end of the reception to the other. Immediately they arrived at the hospital, the Doctor and Nurses started working tirelessly to resuscitate Kike. She was semi-conscious. The parents and siblings were refused entry into the room where she was kept even after much begging. The attending Doctor, a young, lanky and tall individual, who looked too young to be a Doctor, gave firm instruction that no one should be allowed into the room.

They sweated! They prayed! They cried! Dropping herself on the floor of the hospital, Mrs. Johnson called on the Almighty to safe her daughter from whatever had befallen her and to put the plans of the enemy to futility. "What could be wrong with her?" Mr. Johnson asked repeatedly. He expected no answer from anyone in particular. "She showed no sign of sickness before now."

It is the enemies at work," Mrs. Johnson replied. She had turned to a wreck within the space of few minutes of waiting. There was no manifestation of her bravado. Sighting the Medical Director of the hospital, a fellow Deacon at the Church coming from outside, they rushed at him.

"Good afternoon Deacon," Mrs. Johnson greeted, panting. "We don't know what is wrong with her. A Doctor and some Nurses have been with her for a while."

"Calm down," the Doctor responded and adjusted the stethoscope around his neck. He turned to Mr. Johnson and said, "Deacon, all will be well. I was at a meeting when I received your call. Immediately, I called the Doctor on call to assess and start treatment on her. I will go in now and see how she's fairing."

"Thank you sir. Can we?" Mr. Johnson pointed towards the room.

"No!" the Doctor shook his head. "Just give us more time."

Not long after he entered into the room, the door opened with force and Kike was wheeled out looking lifeless. The Medical director followed suit, giving instructions. "Deacon Johnson please follow me," he said. "We need to carry out an urgent evacuation on her in the mini- theatre."

"Evacuation? Of what? Mrs. Johnson shouted holding the Doctor.

"There's no time for long explanation, as we are at risk of losing her. I need you to sign this consent for the procedure to be done." He passed a form to the father. "We will also need a blood donor because, she will definitely need to be transfused."

"We are of same blood group," Mr. Johnson responded.

"Please move to the lab for urgent grouping and cross matching." The Doctor entered into a room marked 'mini theatre' and left them bewildered.

Kike was returned after an hour. Reassuring them that she was out of the blues and would likely make a complete recovery, the Doctor requested that the parents meet him in his office. He looked closely at Mr. & Mrs. Johnson and broke the news they had anxiously been waiting for. "Deacon and Deaconess," he started, "it is so saddening to tell you that, the procedure carried out on your daughter was an evacuation."

"Evacuation? You said it before, but of what?"

The Doctor removed his glasses and placed them on the table. Picking a pen, he made a show of writing on a pad before him, then passed what he wrote to the Johnsons.

They both stood up on reading what was on the paper.

"Abortion?"

"Abortion!"

"Yes!" the Doctor nodded. "Kike had an abortion which was badly done. I don't know what she used. Possibly, a quack might have carried out the procedure on her. There were lots of retained product of conception in her womb, which made her to bleed profusely, likely for days."

"Oh my God! My own daughter," Mrs. Johnson shouted.

"Factually, the laboratory test showed that the blood in her body was less than 15%. I'm still amazed on how her vital organs were still functioning with a PCV of 10%. She almost killed herself. That she is alive is by the Grace of God. That Grace shouldn't be taken for granted."

Mrs. Johnson felt as if the ground should open and swallow her. Frantically looking for where to bury her head, she found none. "God!" she questioned, "If you will disgrace me, must it be in front of a Church member? A Deacon for that matter. Removing her head tie, she used it to clean the sweat that had gathered on her face, then started fanning herself. The air conditioner could not cool the hot air emanating from her. On the other hand, her husband was calm and collected, with a look not betraying his inner thoughts. Thanking the Doctor, he asked what the next line of action would be.

"She should be awake by now," the Doctor responded. "We will monitor her for about three days, to know if she's getting better. She has been placed on antibiotics to combat infection. We will check her blood volume after the transfusion."

Mr. Johnson thanked the Doctor, then excused himself to go and settle the bill, not minding to talk to his wife.

The wife sat glued to the seat, as shame would not allow her stand up. There was palpable silence long after her husband's departure. The Doctor ignored her. Finally, she managed to rise. But instead of leaving the room, she went round the table and knelt before the elderly Doctor asking, "Deacon, what do we do now?"

"Do?" he said. "I told you, she will be okay."

"I'm talking about the Church," she stammered.

"What about the Church?" he asked irritably. "Madam please stand up." He knew where she was heading to, but wouldn't assist her in getting there. The law of karma, he thought and smiled. The Almighty Deaconess has now become a jelly fish. Checking his watch, he informed her that he had a crucial meeting in few minutes, and wouldn't be in the hospital if not for her family.

"Deacon, can I make a request?"

"Feel free."

"I want all that happened this afternoon to be between us. She made a frantic to and fro movement with her right hand. "Please help in covering my shame," she pleaded.

The Doctor looked at her squarely and shook his head before answering. "Madam, it is ethically wrong to divulge the information of my patient to a third party. I would be breaching a professional ethic by telling anyone about what happened today. So, your secret is safe with me."

"Ha! Thank God. Thank you," she smiled. "Thank God," she repeated and prepared to leave the consultation room. The Doctor's deep baritone held her back.

"Why the sudden joy?" he asked. "Not telling anyone would not subtract from the fact that, your daughter committed an act that almost took her life."

"We will discuss that when she gets well. It's a mistake which she will never repeat. The most important thing now is my..."

"Reputation," the Doctor supplied.

"Yes! How will it sound? To hear that my daughter, my own daughter got pregnant and even aborted. What will people say about me?"

"Hmm, you see life? The other day when the case of Mrs. Aboderin's daughter came up, you felt as if you were the Almighty and the only perfect mother on earth. You made it look as if you knew it all. You condemned her, condemned the mother and couldn't hide the fact that you were out to carry out a personal vendetta. You enjoy going around the Church like a police officer, monitoring other peoples' children and leaving your own garden untended. You felt that you could merely protect your children just by being strict. You did not build a formidable wall around them because, you were busy meddling in others affairs. You've forgotten that, those that live in glass houses should not throw stones. Now that the serpent has pushed through a crack and bitten one of yours, I hope you will make amend."

"I'm still concerned about what people will say."

"That is our problem. We get so concerned about what people say, so full of ego, that we don't mind sinning against God. You are concerned about your reputation now, but will be the first to pass instant judgment on others. What you feared most has befallen you. What will you do?"

"Humph."

"Remember Achan that stole the sacred things in the Bible. He thought his sin was covered, until God exposed him and he implicated his household. Remember David and how God dealt with him because of his secret sins. Our sins will always find us out. The Bible says he who covers his sins shall not prosper, but he who confess and forsake them will have mercy. You will be laying a foundation of a lifetime of deception and guilt for your daughter if you let this go."

"What do you suggest I do?"

"Talk to her and let her go to God in full repentance. Inform the Pastor of what happened, and be ready to face the music. Your daughter should take responsibility for what she did, so that she won't repeat it again. Then, continue praying for God to give her the ability to say no to immorality because, no one can prevail by mere human strength and wisdom. I pray God will help you to do the right thing."

TWELVE

Life became unbearable for Martha to the extent that she felt like giving up. The attitude of people towards her- her parents inclusive, made it look as if she was the worst sinner in the world. Her parents were unyielding, unloving and callous. With her father refusing to visit, her mother continually accused Martha of destabilizing her home and setting discord in an otherwise happy marriage. She became bitter to the point of resenting her.

To make matters worse, Mrs. Aboderin became a laughing stock to all and sundry. She returned home from Church at most times in tears because, one person or the other had made a reckless utterance, cast a stone at her or, reacted to her negatively. That was bad for her already fragile mental health and translated in different kinds of physical maladies. She became a recluse and continually transferred aggression on Martha. She only spoke to her in mono syllables.

Martha wanted companionship but no one was there to give to her. She wanted hope but her future looked bleak. Anytime she sat and ruminated on her predicament, she would remember her father's exact words- You have used your hand to ruin your future. You will never amount to anything in life. Furthermore, he said he was glad that she wasn't the only child. He was optimistic that the other children would bring glory to the family name. She constantly remembered those words, until they became part and parcel of her and she started living them. Her talks, thoughts, dressing and demeanor depicted utter hopelessness.

Martha wanted someone to hold her and speak peace to her. She wanted a shoulder to lean on, and a balm to soothe her frayed nerves. The symptoms of pregnancy did not make things easy.

There were times she would throw up, to the extent of almost passing out and all her mother would say was- use avomine, take bitter cola. It got to a point that she felt her Mum was wishing her to die, and she in turn wished her fetus would die and free her. Free her to live a normal life, free her to move on, free her to re-awaken hope and free her to go back to the way she was; a vibrant, young and optimistic lady.

She wished to wake up from the long sleep that she had been subjected to. She wanted to be in the choir singing. She wanted to be in the congregation, not as a caricature in front of the Church, to listen to the Pastor teach about life. She wanted to stand in front of the children and take them on Bible lessons. But no one would allow her sing in the choir, or teach in the Sunday school. She could neither mingle with the unmarried ladies, nor be allowed in the midst of the married.

Martha had become a tainted woman, a scarlet lady that would live the rest of her life in regret, so her father said. Like Tamar, she would die in her father's house as an old maid. He said she wouldn't get a good man to marry her because, no sane man would marry someone with a bastard child.

She expected the Church to delegate someone to counsel her. The Pastor tried, but the person delegated was full of himself. He taught like the Pharisees of those days would do. So Martha stopped seeing him, and he was too glad to be relieved of the duty.

Martha tried turning to the Holy Spirit for help, after she had blamed God for abandoning her to her predicament and letting her enemies gloat over her, but her heart was closed to the gentle voice of the Spirit reassuring her that all will be well.

She developed resentment against God, her family, Jide, Kike, the Church and the whole world. She became extremely bitter, to the point that she stopped having her quiet time. And then, she began wishing for death. After the wish came the actualization. Solitude, a knife, to cut across the wrist. She left a note for her parents.

THIRTEEN

Mrs. Johnson spent weeks brooding over the issue of Kike's misdemeanor. She came up with different reasons to justify herself on why the Pastor mustn't know of what happened to her daughter. How will I tell him? She asked. What will happen to the new position as the coordinator of the virgins' club? She equally asked. To Mrs. Johnson, honor and position meant everything, and she would do anything to gain and retain respect. She weighed the pros and cons and got to the conclusion that, the Pastor must not know.

The issue almost led to a fight between her and her husband, who for once was bent on asserting his authority as the Head of the household. He insisted on doing what was right no matter the consequence. He had to bow to pressure after relentless fire from his wife.

One evening, Mrs. Johnson invited Mrs. Williams and her son Jide to the house for a meeting. It was a closed door meeting between the four, without the knowledge of the fathers. There, she revealed what happened to Kike to the two. Before then, she had claimed Kike had a severe case of malaria and typhoid fever. Looking at Jide in the eyes she said, "You can't deny you did this one."

Jide dropped his head dejectedly.

"Why are you defiling our girls?" she asked.

"Girl you mean?"

"Girls," she repeated. "You know what I mean. Why are you allowing the devil to use you?"

"I'm sorry ma," he pleaded.

"Sorry my foot. Look, this will be the last time you will try this. My daughter almost died from the drug you gave her to induce abortion."

"Jesus!" Mrs. Williams shouted.

"She told me all that I needed to know. She told me it was the second abortion, in the space of three months."

"Ore, sorry," Mrs. Williams pleaded on her knees. Why did you have to go to that extent Jide?"

"The issue is this," Mrs. Johnson stated. "Because my daughter was defiled and had a complicated abortion, Jide should know that he has gotten himself a future wife. With the abortion, we don't know the state of things in Kike's body system. Though the doctor gave assurance that there will be no problem, but who knows what might come up in the future?"

"No evil will happen in Jesus name," Mrs. Williams prayed.

"Amen! But I insist that he has gotten himself a wife. At least if there is problem in the future, they will bear the consequence together. Thank God he's already a graduate, while she will soon be in the high institution. I wouldn't mind them getting married even in her hundred level. Moreover, I don't want my daughter to have to give long explanations of how she was broken to another man."

"I was not the one that deflowered her," Jide grumbled.

"Hen?" Mrs. Williams said in surprise.

"Yes! She was exposed before we met. I'm not under any obligation to marry anybody. I will marry whosoever I want at the right time."

Kike, who had all along sat like a dummy, seeming unconcerned with all that was going on around her, looked up at Jide sorrowfully. "Jide!" She called, "Your promise was that you will marry me. It is why I have been giving my body to you. Why are you saying this?" Kike looked pitiful, pathetic and disheveled, with the ordeal she had undergone showing on her emaciated body.

"What's even the certainty that I was responsible for your pregnancy?" Jide asked. "I'm not under obligation to marry anybody," he repeated. "I will marry whosoever I want at the right time."

"And you will rot in jail," Mrs. Johnson threatened. "If you don't behave, the Pastor will get to know that indeed, you raped Martha. My daughter confessed to me that it was true she visited you and met Martha at the gate to your house on the day you raped her. You had sex with my daughter before releasing her to go back to the coaching center. She was suspicious of what could happen between you and Martha so, she went back, peeped through a break in the glass door and waited long enough to see you forcing yourself on her."

"Ha!" Mrs. Williams exclaimed.

"If you don't behave," Mrs. Johnson continued, "all I will do is to expose your evil deeds to the Pastor."

"I'm ready to own up," Jide responded and stood up. "I have not been at peace since the day Martha was punished. I will own up and take responsibility for the pregnancy. Martha is a decent girl. More so, I was her first man."

"Go ahead," Mrs. Johnson said and pointed to her friend. "Your son will rot in jail. You think Professor Aboderin will take it lightly with you? After the humiliation that you put his family through. I will tell you if you don't know. The penalty for rapists as it is, is 14 years jail term. You better sit down and hear me out."

Jide sat back terrified, looking towards his mother for help. She was equally terrified. She pacified Mrs. Johnson on her knees. "Ore, we are sorry," she said. "We will do whatever you want."

"Fine. The two of them must get married at a set time. You know Kike is my only daughter. Don't you think I also want to be called by the Pastor the morning after their wedding? – To receive the news that my daughter's husband called to say he met her at home. Don't you like the way the Pastor's wife praise mothers whose daughters are found chaste? I also want that honor, and this union will guarantee that. I know your son will not dream of eating excreta. He should never think of backing out because as my people will say, a pounded yam of twenty years can remain hot on one's palm.

"What about my grandchild in Martha's womb?" Mrs. Williams asked. "Now that we know that Jide had his way with her. Will it be right to allow her face the consequence alone?"

"You can go to the Church and announce that you are now a grandmother, and see how your son will waste away. If Prof. refuses to press charges, I will personally report that Jide also raped my daughter. You better borrow yourself sense."

They agreed that Jide and Kike would marry in the nearest future. Before the Williams left, Mrs. Johnson gave a stern warning to Jide. Pointing at him she said, "Go and learn how to control your instrument. Make sure you tie it with rope, wire, cord, anything, until when you will be ready to father another child. Omo iran Kiran."

FOURTEEN

An angel prevented Martha from committing suicide. As she was about severing the radial artery that would make life drain out of her via bright red blood, a knock sounded on the door, and she dropped the knife in confusion. She had forgotten to lock it in her haste to get things done and face whatever eternity held for her. She never even thought anyone could be around at that time, to come and knock on the door.

The person at the door refused to go away. Martha also refused to stand up. She sat on her buttocks with legs spread wide, staring pointedly at a spot, as if she had already seen the spirit of death. With repeated knockings without response, the door was opened by the knocker; an elderly, plump and nice matronly looking woman, with the characteristic Christian - mother fleshy arm.

She was surprised at Martha, who continued looking at the same spot, oblivious to her entry. Moving towards her, she assessed the situation; Martha in a trance like posture, the kitchen knife beside her and the note, which she scanned through at a glance.

She bent towards her and drew her up, taking her small frame into her large one. As Martha's head rested on her chest, she felt a kind of warmth she had long longed for, a welcome home, a motherly bosom. Emotions overran Martha and she burst into uncontrollable tears; venting, pouring, washing her innermost of all that was bottled inside. The woman allowed her to cry and even offered the edge of her wrapper to clean her face afterwards. She wasn't in anyway concerned that Martha was soiling her wrapper with catarrh from the nostrils.

Mrs. Ndukwe was a neighbor to the Aboderins'. She was a spirit- filled child of God; who promptly acted on the nudging of the Holy Spirit to knock on the door. She was glad that she did not disobey. She allowed Martha to cry, then led her to her house. It was the next flat. She offered her a hot cup of tea and a plate of well prepared, steaming catfish pepper soup. Martha ate like a wolf. She confessed that she had been craving for pepper soup for a long time. Mrs. Ndukwe explained to her that, craving for different varieties of food is part of the issues of pregnancy. She said that Martha could always come to her for anything.

That encounter heralded the beginning of an enduring mother and daughter relationship between the two. Martha found solace in the fact that, Mrs. Ndukwe was a mother to the core. With all her children married and out of the family nest, she saw Martha as a gift from God to nurture, until she could stand on her feet again.

Martha not only benefited from her deep spiritual knowledge emanating from a close relationship with God, but also from her versatility in different skills like baking, bead making, tailoring and decoration. Mrs. Ndukwe was a replica of the virtuous woman in Proverbs 31; she possessed all required qualities. Mrs. Ndukwe became Martha's mentor.

With them getting closer, Martha made her home a second home. Mrs. Aboderin was too glad to get someone that would relieve her of Martha's problem. Martha on her part, was never tired of asking questions, and sitting silently to learn from Mrs. Ndukwe on daily basis. Mrs. Ndukwe would tell her that, "It is the duty of every parent to train and bring the child up in the fear of the Lord. Though, many lack the know-how. Even those that know what to do are often too busy to create time for the children. Some claim they are engaged in Church activities, not knowing that the home is the first mission field of the parents."

"Did you allow your children have friends of the opposite

sex when they were growing up?" Martha asked during a discussion on child upbringing.

Mrs. Ndukwe smiled and said, "I wasn't scared of my children having friends but, I made sure they were involved in healthy relationships. I and Daddy personally led our children to Christ at very early age. The desire for the children to know Christ, should always be paramount in the mind of every parent. We are often preoccupied with the need for them to go to the best schools, wear the best clothes, eat the best foods, that we forget the most important need."

"The most important need?"

"The salvation of their souls. It has been established that, 84% of people make the decision to follow Christ between the ages of 4 and 14. Only about 10% make the decision between ages 15 and 30."

"Interesting."

"It is better when you catch them young. You know, when a child is in God and you plant the word of God in his heart," Mrs. Ndukwe said, pointing towards her heart, "The child will know that God has a purpose for his existence. At every junction of decision making; having a life partner, choosing a career, choosing friends and even when tempted, the individual will always wait on God to know his perfect will."

"I see," Martha nodded.

"Things were easier for me and Daddy because, we are both born again. We have the same principles about God, about religion and about child upbringing. After leading our children to Christ, we kept nurturing them in the truth of the word of God. All the while, we did not spare the rod. We used the rod whenever necessary, and used the word at all times. We never got tired of praying for them. I want you to know today that, what men of valor wouldn't achieve by their strength, a prayerful woman can achieve on her knees."

"Wonderful!"

"We allowed them to socialize, while setting boundaries. We also gave them sound sex education."

"You taught them about sex?"

"Yes! We started by making them know the proper names for sexual organs, and knowing the key differences between the male and the female gender. Before attaining puberty, we prepared them for what to expect and what to do with sexual urge. We made them realize the dangers in premarital sex, phonography, masturbation and other vices.

"Oh God! Martha exclaimed, "My Mum never taught me all that, except telling me that I must remain a virgin, if I want to have a white wedding. She emphasized on white wedding so much, that I thought it was a ticket to enter heaven."

"Well, it is possible your Mum lacked the knowledge of how to go about it. I see people getting into marriages, without proper education on child upbringing. Parents especially the mothers, must have good knowledge of raising children. What you don't have, you can't give. On the issue of virginity, I'm an advocate of sexual purity and not just an intact hymen."

"How do you mean?"

"Thanks for asking. There are countless young people who are going about, that are technically virgins, but are sexually dirty. They engage in all sort of dirty activities like oral and anal sex, masturbation, phonography and even homosexuality. Their mind is depraved and dirty but, they still go around claiming virginity. Someone who had been sexually active, had repented and vowed to remain pure, is better than them. Sexual purity is the in thing."

"I was once like that," Martha confessed.

"Thank God for your life," Mrs. Ndukwe responded. "I hope you will remain in the joy and peace that Christ has given you."

"Amen! All your children must have turned out well,"

Martha concluded.

"Yes they did, but it wasn't easy. Even with all the trainings and prayers, our last baby derailed.

"What?"

"The enemy is always after the children of God, especially when he sees their glorious future. Our last child went wayward in the University and got pregnant for a fellow student."

"What did you do?"

"We had no choice but to lead her back to Christ. We supported and encouraged her. She deferred a year at the University, delivered her baby, went back to face her studies squarely and came out as a first class graduate of Nursing science."

"Incredible!"

"She later got married to the father of her baby, after he gave his life to Christ. They are settled in the UK and doing well."

Martha fell into silence after the conversation, and Mrs. Ndukwe knew something was bothering her. She probed until Martha voiced out. "Is there any hope for me?" she asked with a shaky voice. "My Dad said I'm hopeless."

"Oh mine!" Mrs. Ndukwe cried and took her into her arms, soothing her like one would a baby. "You are not hopeless," she said and jerked Martha up. Looking at her directly and pointing a finger she said, "Hear the word of God. Job 14:7-9- For there is hope of a tree, if it be cut down, that it will sprout again, and that the tender branch thereof will not cease. Though the root thereof wax old in the earth, and the stock thereof die in the ground; yet through the scent of water it will bud, and bring forth boughs like a plant. You are like that plant! You will bud! You will bring forth fruits and fulfil God's purpose. Go forth and bask in the glory of God."

FIFTEEN

Kike got admission into the University of her Choice to study Biochemistry. Her utmost joy was in the realization that, she would have the chance to live a free and unchaperoned life; a life devoid of parental restrictions, a life to be lived to the fullest, and a life she had always dreamt of. She would do whatever she like, go wherever she want, and shake off her shackles of bondage. She might need to sieve her clique of friends, since she will now be a "big girl."

To her, tertiary institution meant unrestricted access to the good life. No one would force her to cook, eat and go to Church or dress in a specific way, since she would be living away from home. She would have to make her own decisions.

Her parents gave the usual advice before she left home and listed additional rules to be obeyed. Reminding her of what had happened before, they made her promise she wouldn't disappoint them again and soil the family name. On her own, Mrs. Johnson reminded her of the agreement between her and Jide. Drawing her ear she said, "Ai moko omo, ka tun male re. You must remain true to Jide."

"I will ma," Kike responded.

"You must not allow what happened before to happen again. Strive to ensure you remain qualified for a white wedding."

"I will ma."

After the abortion episode of months back, Kike had realized the development of a stronger desire to satisfy the flesh, but she was scared of getting pregnant again. Therefore, she resulted to the use of contraceptives. There were times she wished, that things had turned out differently. Maybe her life wouldn't be the way it was, if her mother was loving and attentive, if her father was firm and outspoken, if God and not religious doctrines and philosophies was allowed to rule her home.

Settling in the campus wasn't easy, with the registration, orientation, lectures and other activities taking their toll on her. Kike realized she had no grooming for an independent life and she suffered. She soon found her feet and began living the kind of life she wanted.

Ditching her conservative wears, Kike opted for trendy clothes that were in vogue; topless, bottomless and see- through. She seldom attended fellowship, but pitched her tent with the "happening babes" on campus. Like a bird freed from a cage, she flapped her wings and flew far beyond her boundary. Needless to say that, she was still that religious and well behaved girl whenever she returned home. Parents would often point her out to their children, as an example of what a Christian youth should be.

Kike needed a man to continue servicing her in school. A man who would not make her feel the absence of Jide; who was serving his father land in Calabar. Calabar is a city of about 720 kilometers to Jos where she was schooling. She decided to seek for an alternative. With an insatiable urge for sex, Kike became indiscriminate in her choices of men. She went for anything in trousers. And who would tell her parents? Her school was a little distanced from Kaduna, where her parents lived. Not too far for parents to visit their kid, someone would say. Mr. & Mrs. Johnson were content to put her under the care of a guardian, a supposed Christian they met at a denominational conference. In no time, he became another sexual partner to Kike. Albeit to say that, he would always give false reports of her good conducts and disciplined lifestyle to the parents.

In one way or the other, Jide got to know about her

activities. He visited without prior notice and discovered that she was co-habiting with a student staying off campus, a habit that has eaten deep into the fabrics of many undergraduates.

If a good number of parents knew what their children and wards do behind them, especially in tertiary institutions, they would shed hot and bitter tears. A significant percentage of students are single at home, and act married in school, living with sexual partners. It will take the Grace of God for such not to lose focus. It always seemed as if, the higher institution is a world on its own, where immorality is seen as the norm and everyone struggles to join the bandwagon.

Nevertheless, there are always remnants that wouldn't defile themselves, like Daniel and Joseph in the foreign land. They won't get carried away, like 'Dinah', by going out to watch 'the ladies of the land.' Those remnants won't feed fat on the delicacies of Babylon, knowing it has the ability to weaken and cause spiritual insensitivity and apathy. They won't dare Potiphar's wife, since they know she's a fire that could burn and rob them of their glorious future. They are focused, godly and reliable. Even while on campus, they gladly combine their academic activities with Kingdom business.

Jide saw Kike's actions as an opportunity to pull out from the planned future pact, but Kike was also ready for him. Unknowingly to him, she had a contact monitoring him where he was serving. The contact gave her blow to blow account of his frolicking with different ladies. The disagreement that ensued as a result of the discoveries could best be imagined. It became glaring that any future marriage between them would be a disaster.

SIXTEEN

Martha dug deep into the well of Grace. She got herself drunk with the living water that could quench every thirst. Since the word of God gave the mandate for his children to rise and shine, she took God at his word and began to radiate his glory.

She was radiating the glory, as she carried the pregnancy for the remaining months. Still radiating the glory, when she gave birth to baby Testimony. She was full of glory as she engaged in trading activities, to earn what to use to care for her baby, not wanting to place unnecessary burdens on her parents. She would clasp Testimony to her back and sit patiently at a make-shift shop adjacent to a school, waiting for customers to patronize her snacks. She wasn't ashamed of her hustle and resolved within her, that she wouldn't allow anyone to intimidate her.

Her Mum almost blew her top, when she discovered what Martha was doing. "Are you insane?" She asked, pointing at her head. What do you want people to say about us? That you! The daughter of Prof. Aboderin, sits in front of a school to sell snacks. For crying out loud, I personally provide all you and your...need." She dodged mentioning Testimony's name.

"That's the point Mum." Martha took it up from there. "I wouldn't want to always depend on you. Considering the fact that I even have a child, I want to fend for her and not put every burden on you. You are still bitter at me, so it won't sound well for me to be using your money to take care of her."

"Your Dad will not be happy if he comes back and see you doing that. It's degrading."

"No ma," Martha shook her head. "It's rather dignifying

because, there's dignity in labor."

"Okay, okay," her Mum raised her left hand. "I meant to discuss something with you before."

"Yes ma."

"As your parents, we want the best for you, even though you disappointed us. We have decided to give you another chance, but it will be conditional."

"Okay."

"We are willing to sponsor you abroad for your tertiary education. We feel a change of environment will do you good. We want you to put the past behind you."

"My past is already behind me," Martha smiled. "I have moved on with my life."

"Not as a teenage mother selling doughnut." Mrs. Aboderin looked at her disdainfully. "We want you to go and start a new lease of life abroad, but..."

"But what?"

"You have to give up your daughter for adoption."

Martha turned sharply and looked at her mother as if she was seeing a stranger. She held Testimony closely to her chest, as if someone would snatch her away from her. Mrs. Aboderin stood and held her by the shoulder. She pleaded. "It's not a big deal. All we need to do is, look for one of the motherless babies' homes around and make arrangement. There are always families willing to pick up babies like her."

"But she's not motherless. She has a mother that loves her. I will never give her up, even if it means me losing opportunities. I don't care."

"You can't tag her along all your life," her mother cried. "Give her up and live as if she never existed."

"What you are asking me to do is wrong," Martha replied

with tears in her eye. "I will not do it."

The discussion thus ended, with Martha determined more than ever to make something out of her life. She gathered a neat sum and got JAMB form, since she already had a complete WAEC result. Her first JAMB score was not good enough to secure a place at her school of choice. The second attempt was better, but she wasn't given admission. By the third time she wrote JAMB, she scored such a high point, which was unbelievable even to her.

On the day that Martha got admission into the University, she ran home to inform Mrs. Ndukwe; who collected the admission letter and danced round the compound. She released prophecies into the life of Martha and mandated her to tell her parents.

The parents were dumb founded, perplexed and shame-faced, when she told them of her admission to study Guidance and counselling. How did you do it? How manage you were able to score a point that earned you a place at the highly competitive state University? They asked. Martha answered them by reciting Philippians 4:13, that through Christ she can do all things.

Well, they humbled themselves enough to seek for forgiveness, for neglecting and sidelining her when she needed them. They confessed that it was their bruised ego that was pained so much that sought for revenge on her. For the first time since she was born, Prof. Aboderin carried his granddaughter, gushing over how she looked so much like him.

And another thing happened. Martha's parents acknowledged the fact that they had all along been practicing religion without knowing Christ. Martha's life and determination had challenged them, and they also want to start walking with Christ. They were not ashamed to request that their daughter lead them in saying the sinner's prayer, as they gave their lives to Christ.

SEVENTEEN

1, 2, 3 years passed. Life went on as usual at Beulah Salvation Assembly. People came and left. There were several births and few deaths. There were marriages, christenings, dedications and burials. The Church continued to grow in numerical strength, but the spiritual atmosphere was dense. Even with the Pastor trying to bring an all-round revival to the Church, most of the members preferred remaining in their comfort zones of service in the flesh.

Revd. Bamiro had a stroke, but was miraculously healed with no physical disability. He had few years to retirement thus, the Church engaged the services of two associate Pastors. They would be his assistants and possibly take over the rein of leadership at the due time.

One was Revd. Alhassan, a tall, huge and no-nonsense man. He had a method of asserting and hammering on points, until he had his way. With track record of many years in Church planting and administration, he looked like someone that the Church needed at that point in time. Needless to say, majority of the council members were skeptical at his appointment. They voiced out their misgivings, seeing him as someone that would listen to nobody and scatter the Church in little time. On that, Revd. Bamiro stood his ground, maintaining that what the Church needed was someone that would bring change. He had the support of the headquarters, and the council members had to handoff and watch events unfold.

True to their thinking, immediately Revd. Alhassan settled down and with the support of the senior Pastor, he began a process of sanitizing the Church of some perceived abnormalities.

He started by formulating a plan on rotating Deacons, elders and officers that had served the Church for years. Emphasizing that people mustn't 'sit tight' on Church offices, he said every member should be given the privilege to serve. This did not go down well with the old hands, who felt that someone shouldn't just come and start pushing them around.

If not handled well, Church politics could be worse than politics in the secular world. The process of selection of the officers was hijacked by the powers that be, and became riddled with manipulations and backstabbing. Less room was given for prayers, while more was given to favoritism and nepotism. At the end of the day, the motive for the action wasn't achieved. People like Mrs. Johnson and Mrs. Williams were retained as Church officers.

The other associate Pastor was a younger man. He was fresh from the seminary, unmarried and eager to carry out the mandate given to him. His good and youthful look, his simple and open character and his unmarried state, made the congregants think that he wouldn't deliver. But, one just needed to be under his ministration to know the stuff he was made of. Pastor Kayode Olukorede, earned the respect of everyone before long.

It was Revd. Alhassan that was assigned to counsel Jide and Kike, who were finally ready to tie the nuptial knot after years of: monitoring each other bumper to bumper, fighting and settling on an already defiled bed, breaking up and reconciling. Deep within Kike, she knew the foundation of their relationship was too shaky to stand the test of time. She would have loved to opt out, but she was scared of where to start from. Already, she had finished youth service, and had gotten a mouthwatering job with an NGO. Life was good except for the fact that, her relationship was sour.

She had almost told her mum that she wanted out of the relationship, the day she caught Jide in bed with another choir member, a 15-year-old girl. It seemed the devil had commissioned Jide to scatter the lives of young ladies. Kike had almost told her Mum, but the latter had choose that moment to inform her that another Church girl, would be getting married soon. Kike should do Pa! Pa! Pa, and tell Jide to bring his people. In her words, "I had labored for many people. I want to reap the harvest now. Moreover, you are not getting any younger."

So, it seemed Kike had no choice. She wished things were different. She wished she could just garner courage and leave Jide. At 24, she was still young and marketable. Furthermore, there were countless eligible young men around, even in the Church. Men like Pastor Kayode. She started crushing on the first day that she met him. She did all she could to catch his attention to no avail, rather, he was always polite and courteous to her and everybody.

Kike had proposed within her that, if someone like Pastor Kayode made advances at her, she would throw all caution to the wind, disregard her Mum and jump at the opportunity. Her Mum would make the usual noise and later calm down. She would soon be carried away with the euphoria of her daughter getting married to a Pastor. That would mean more power for her.

Well, Pastor Kayode or someone else did not propose, and Kike had to make do with the bird at hand. She earnestly hoped and prayed that Jide would change after their wedding, which had been slated for four months.

Jide and Kike sat before Revd. Alhassan, ready to give already rehearsed answers to questions that would be asked. They had been tutored by their mothers about what to say. The mothers also allayed any fear of retribution that could arise from misleading a man of God. It looked as if the series of deceptions over the years, had hardened the heart of the two mothers-especially Mrs. Johnson. Kike was afraid and hid her trembling palms under her blouse. She prayed that the Pastor wouldn't ask a question that would get her confused and make her say out all that they were hiding.

The Pastor looked intently at them, so intent that, Kike felt he could read into their prepared lies. However, they went ahead to tell him that they were both chaste and had lived clean lives. The Pastor was happy and gladly took them through the Nitti - gritty of what to expect on the wedding night and in marriage generally. The counselling session would be for a month. Revd. Alhassan also made a note to use them as point of reference to the unmarried youths, if he would be the one to preach at their wedding.

While the counselling session was on, Martha drove into the Church in her mother's car to pick her daughter. She had earlier been dropped for a day starlight fellowship camp. Informed that they still had an hour to the end of the camping program, Martha decided to stay it out in the car, with an earpiece fixed to both ears.

She was deeply engrossed in what she was doing, shaking her head to the highly inspiring music of Ayuba Yakubu, when the door gently opened. Removing the earpiece, she starred into the not too familiar face of Pastor Kayode, barely managing to voice out a distorted good evening sir.

"Evening. I tapped on the glass for some time. You were carried away."

"I'm sorry sir. I was listening to a song."

"Who was that?" he pointed to her phone.

"Ayuba Yakubu." He's a Nurse musician. The Album is titled "Yabo", and talks about giving glory to God because, everything belongs to him."

"That's great. Can I?" He pointed to her phone, the ear piece and his ear.

"You mean?"

"Yes please."

Martha got down from the car to stand beside him as he fixed the earpiece on one ear and passed the other end to her. She collected it reluctantly and fixed on her left ear. They sang along with Ayuba.

Daukaka, da iko naka ne

Jehovah san yabe ka

Standing there and listening to the Gospel artiste, one would think they were siblings and not a Pastor and member. With Martha in a simple gown and the Pastor in a white polo atop three quarter jeans, his low cut hair ruffled and uncombed, passers-by gazed at them curiously. When the song ended, Pastor Kayode removed the ear- piece and returned it to her, thanking her in the process. They exchanged numbers.

EIGHTEEN

Pastor Kayode and Martha met again at the Church at his request. Before then, Martha had struggled with lots of conflicting emotions coupled with her inability to erase the memory of the little time they shared when they first met. The Pastor's eyes kept surfacing at all waking and sleeping moments. The depth, the wisdom, the fire in them. They looked familiar, like eyes she had seen before. They exchanged pleasantries, after which Pastor Kayode complimented her on her dressing. Martha blushed and looked away. Not mincing words, he stated his mission to her.

"I first caught a glimpse of you the day I was inducted as an associate Pastor in the Church," he said. "I don't know what drew my attention to you, as I stood to receive the hands of fellowship from the Pastors and elders. I saw a young, beautiful lady holding a child. There was an aura around you that I couldn't explain. Your thought kept reoccurring after the service and thereafter. I started praying because, it seemed God was telling me something."

Martha kept her face straight as the Pastor spoke. She was already preparing a polite rebuff in her mind. What could God have told him? She questioned and smiled slightly. She had erased anything that would have to do with relationship from her life's itinerary. After the rape and the aftermath, she had kept all MEN except her Dad and siblings at arm's length. Martha had rather focused on things that mattered most- her relationship with God, her daughter, her education and family. They came in that order. Her Daughter would be six in a month time. Martha was in 300 level. What is this Pastor saying? She murmured.

"I have been praying since then," she heard him say. "I was indoor last Saturday at the Pastorium, when I had a push to go out.

It was very strong. I knew something pleasant was waiting for me, maybe an answer to a prayer. I obeyed. If you noticed, my hair wasn't combed. I was even in bathroom slippers. When I saw you, I was convinced that you are the one that God has prepared as my wife. I got talking with the Senior Pastor, and he said I should meet you after praying with me. And here I am, to ask you to pray and think about becoming my wife."

Martha took her time in answering. Fidgeting with a button on her hand bag, she sighed and stated emphatically, "I don't think you heard God clearly."

"How do you mean? Why did you say that? He was surprised.

"Because he knows I don't need a husband," Martha answered boldly. "I don't want marriage, and I want to be left alone." She turned her back to move away, but Pastor Kayode's next words stopped her.

"Don't be rude Martha. At least, you can pray about the proposal, even if you don't want it."

Martha frowned her face and asked, "Why will God want you to marry me?"

"Who are you" Pastor Kayode asked gently. He focused on her face.

"Hmm!" Martha breathed deeply. "I'm my simple self. I'm a child of God but, I have an ugly past. Although I had waded through waters and fires to ensure my past doesn't interfere with my future, there's no how a scar can ever be like a normal flesh."

"You are speaking in parables Martha."

"Pastor! I know you must have heard of my story. That child you saw with me the first day you noticed me, is my flesh and blood. She has no father. I have resolved to use the rest of my life taking care of her, and serving God faithfully. I don't want marriage."

Pastor Kayode folded his arms across his chest, looked straight at Martha and prayed for God to give him the wisdom to get across to her. Gently he said, "I strongly know you are the will of God for my life. I have no doubt about it. I have also developed a kind of fondness for you. I just wish you will pray. At least pray."

"Pastor," Martha cut in, "The Bible tells me in the book of Leviticus 21:7, that a priest should not marry a harlot; or a woman who has been defiled; neither shall they marry a woman divorced from her husband; for the priest is holy unto him God. You see! I will be doing you a disservice by even promising to pray about the proposal, because I won't."

"Why?' the Pastor asked.

"Let's face reality. I might be a clog in the wheel of your progress as a minister, if you marry me. Other ministers would look down on you, for marrying someone who already has a child. If you remain in this Church, you might even be denied the right to become a senior Pastor. I have a child, a child that the father wouldn't acknowledge. I beg you to let ..."

"Sister Martha," Pastor Kayode called quietly.

"You need an untouched woman," she continued. "Someone that has never been with a man. Someone like Mary. She was used as a vessel to bring forth our savior because, she was pure and chaste."

"Martha! Look at me. Have you finished your bible exposition?"

She smiled.

"It is true that Mary was used as a vessel to bring forth Christ. It is true that she was a virgin. But then, in the same lineage of Christ, there were women that were not so worthy, but God used them as worthy vessels because of their willingness."

"Agreed."

"Who would have thought that Rahab, a harlot, from a

heathen country, would find Grace before God to be in Christ's lineage? At least, you've never been a harlot."

"Never."

"Who would have thought that Ruth, a Moabite, a country whose people mustn't enter the house of God, would find Grace? She was also included in the lineage of Christ. Bathsheba became David's wife through manipulation and bloodshed. She also found Grace. At a point in their lives, God choose them to become vessels unto honor. Moreover, the Bible said in the book of Romans 8:30 that- those that God predestinate, them he also called: and those he called, he also justified; and those he justified, he also glorified. Martha! No matter your past, you are a glorious woman. I see it in you."

Martha felt peace descending on her as the Pastor continued.

"As for my ministerial progression that you mentioned, it is in the hands of God. He called me and knows where he will lead me. Nothing can ever stand in my way, if I remain in his will."

"Sure!"

"Furthermore, I have heard about your past but it doesn't move me an inch. I see your present and I love who you are. Everyone has a past, either good or bad. Our victory lies in the ability not to allow our past to mar the future. When we dwell too much on the past, it becomes a barrier to God operating in our lives. For you in particular, God wants to use the mess of your past to give a great message to the world. I hope you will allow him."

"What of my child?" Martha asked. "I have a child."

"I know," Pastor Kayode answered. "I know you have a child that is as beautiful as you are. God knows you have a child, when he made me realize you are my missing rib. I would gladly accept her as mine if we become one."

"I don't know what to do," Martha lamented. "Will it be right to accept your proposal? Am I worthy to be a Pastor's wife?

After all that had happened. I have always seen Pastors' wives as honorable women with great assignments. I was made to know that I wouldn't be worthy for a single man because of my child. I was equally advised to focus on marrying a widower or a divorcee. I made a resolution to remain single for life. I choose to train my daughter alone. But here you are, asking me to be your wife. I haven't even graduated from the University. I see eligible, single and ready ladies in the Church, as well as vibrant sisters, but God directed you to me, a mother of a child that the Father won't acknowledge."

"That is Grace. My sister, Grace. It is the ability of God, at man's disposal. I want you to pray about the proposal," Pastor Kayode pleaded. "I will give you as much time as you want but please, don't keep me waiting."

"I will pray and get back to you, as soon as I have what to tell you," she answered with drops of tears.

"I know God will guide you but, the choice remains yours. Even if you won't accept my proposal, I respect you a lot. You will always occupy a special place in my heart. Cheer up!" He touched her lightly on the cheek. "You are a strong woman."

After that, they walked side by side to the gate. Suddenly, Martha remembered something and stopped. Facing the Pastor she said, "Your surname sounds familiar."

"It is a common name."

"Yes but, there's something about the...I think I remember now. There was a revivalist that came here years ago. That must be the name."

"You mean a vibrant, fiery old man with grey hairs at the temple and a dark birth mark on the nose."

"Wait Pastor, did you know him?"

"What do you think?" Pastor Kayode teased her.

"Wait! Your face, don't tell me."

"He happened to be my father."

"Oh my God!" Martha screamed, then covered her mouth as the scream had attracted women who were cleaning the Church compound, with Mrs. Johnson and Mrs. Williams seated and directing them. They looked curiously at the two.

"I gave my life to Christ under his ministration," Martha said.

"You don't mean it."

"I wish to meet him again," she said excitedly.

"You will. As his daughter-in-law." Pastor Kayode smiled.

"Why are you so sure of this?"

"Because God has said it and I believe it. I can also see it in your eyes, that your answer will be a yes."

Mrs. Johnson glided to the Pastor's office. Knocking vigorously, she entered and dumped herself into a chair. Revd. Bamiro looked at her curiously, waiting for a word from her.

"I saw something disturbing outside," she said when she finally found her voice.

"Disturbing?"

"This is not the first time I'm seeing them together."

"Who?" The Pastor asked.

"Pastor Kayode should put himself in a state of honor and stop sending wrong signals to the youths."

"How? What did he do?"

"This is the second time I'm see him having deep conversations with that girl," Mrs. Johnson tightened her mouth.

"What girl?"

"That one that gave birth to the child without a father."

"You mean Martha?"

"That is her name."

Revd. Bamiro turned his chair round and brought his face at par with Mrs. Johnson's saying, "Pastor Kayode is an adult and knows what is good for him. Have a nice day Madam. Eku imura iyawo."

NINETEEN

With the past behind them, though some happenings still reminded them of a past that wouldn't erase totally from peoples' minds, the Aboderins moved on with life. The peace and harmony that was earlier lost came back into being.

One day, one time, Martha sat close to her Mum in the living room. They were having a mother- daughter conversation. Prof. Aboderin sat at a few meters away. He was keen on a football match replay.

Martha cleared her throat and said, "Dad, Mum, I have something to tell you."

"Hun-Hun," Prof. murmured. He was deeply engrossed in what he was watching.

"Okay," his wife responded.

"God is leading me towards starting a ministry for young ladies, especially rape victims, pregnant teenagers, single mothers and women that are generally neglected, ostracized and seen as the worst sinners.

"Beautiful," Mrs. Aboderin replied enthusiastically. "That's a good one.

"Ministry?" Prof. said absentmindedly. He wasn't still concentrating.

Mrs. Aboderin stood up, picked the TV remote and pressed a button. Phew! The TV went off. Prof. stood up and shook his head saying, "I'm at the mercy of the two of you now. Let my boys come back. We will deal with you."

"We are also ready for you," his wife replied jokingly and

drew Martha close. "I think we should listen to Martha. She's making a good point."

Martha repeated herself and spoke passionately. She said she was fully convinced that God wanted her to work with the downtrodden and ostracized women in the society. "With what I experienced and see in the Church and the society at large," she said. "We have a long way to go in relating and reaching out to people who found themselves in one fault or the other, especially when it has to do with sexual sins. It's not a crime to preach against sexual sins. It's not a crime to discipline people who fall at one time or the other. But, it is a great crime to throw sinners away without offering any support."

"That's what we do," Mrs. Aboderin cut in. "We throw them to a world that doesn't care a hoot for them. I know better now."

"We often forget that, Christ came not for only the healthy, but for sinners. He also mandated us to love everyone equally. I want to create a platform where we will show genuine love and help the lost and confused to find their feet again."

"That's a good initiative, "Prof. said. "As your parents, we will partner with you and give needed support, for you to fulfil God's purpose for your life."

"Yes!" Mrs. Aboderin added, "I will also give added support on my knees."

Prof. suddenly went silent then whispered, 'Martha."

"Yes Dad," she responded and focused on him.

"There's something I have always wanted to ask. I don't know how you will take it."

"Fire on Dad."

"About Jide. Even after many years, I'm yet to come to terms that you could do all...were you really raped or...?"

Martha took a long time in answering. When she was ready, two big tears dropped from her eyeballs. She wiped them with the back of her right palm, while her Mum drew her into a warm embrace saying, "We've always wanted to know. If you are not ready to..." she shrugged.

"I am ready," Martha replied and sat up straight, "Yes! Jide raped me. After the encounter I had at the revival, I decided to cut off the unholy relationship between us."

"Unholy relationship?"

"Yes. We were dating in secret. We were doing diverse filthy acts unworthy of Christians, apart from vaginal sex. The reason why we were not having vaginal sex was because, I wanted to preserve my virginity at all cost. We were fornicating but technically, I was a virgin."

"Hun!" the Prof. sighed deeply.

"Jide had me where he wanted. I shouldn't have gone to his house in the first place. I should just have left it at quitting the relationship. I think one part of me still harbored the hope that Jide would change, promise that he would wait for me and then, marry me in the future. Many young people still fall into the same kind of trap. They feel they have the future in their hands and can structure it in any way they want. Many have lost out because they lack intimacy with the owner of the future. Parents, the Church and the society have a lot to do because, things are already out of hand. I fell for Jide's lies and manipulations, just as many gullible and vulnerable girls are falling. I have found my feet because Grace found me. It's unfortunate that, it might not be so for others. They might not get the help they need on time."

"Jide is a devil incarnate," Mrs. Aboderin stood and screamed. "See the way he concocted the lies to the extent that, even we couldn't believe our daughter."

"He has to pay for his crime," Prof vowed. "I will definitely resurrect the matter."

"No Dad please," Martha begged on her knees. "I also thought that way until the Holy Spirit ministered to me that I should leave it. He said every secret thing will be made open at the due time."

"At the due time?"

"Yes Dad. At the due time."

At the mention of the word 'time', a knock sounded at the door and Prof. asked if Martha was expecting a visitor.

"Oh! She exclaimed and placed a palm on her chest. "I invited a friend to meet you today."

"A friend?"

Martha nodded.

The friend was Pastor Kayode. He came in with his usual tension-relieving smile. Greeting the parents, he whispered to Martha. "Hope am not late." Martha shook her head and blushed. Both parents were surprised and felt the wave passing between the two. It was physically glaring that there was something going on. They listened attentively to what Martha had to say.

"Dad! Mum!" she began. "I invited Pastor K. here. About a month ago, he proposed marriage to me. I told him to give me time to pray. After getting the confirmation that he's God's choice for me, I accepted his proposal last week and invited him to the house today, knowing that you both will be around."

After Martha was done speaking, Pastor Kayode stood and prostrated flat in front of the Prof. who quickly stood and raised him up. "Don't do that Pastor," he begged.

"It is necessary Sir," Pastor Kayode said. "The Bible says we should give honor to whom it is due. More so, Martha is worth more, and I will give more than this, if only to be allowed to court my beloved." He looked at Martha affectionately and said, "I love her Sir. I am 100% sure she's God's choice for me. I seek for your permission to court her. I am ready to wed her in the most nearest future."

"I thought Pastors were trained to hide their emotions," Mrs. Aboderin joked.

"Some emotions cannot be hidden ma," Pastor Kayode replied. "Moreover, Pastors are also human, with the ability to love and to hate. Because we are children of God, his love is shed abroad in our hearts. So, we have a large capacity to love. God helping us to become man and wife, I will ensure that I love, cherish and care for her with the totality of my being. Not even our children will get the kind of love I'd show to her."

"Oh Martha! You got the best," Mrs. Aboderin cried and wiped tears from her face.

"Yes daughter," Prof also said. "Your man has thrown a challenge to me. I think your Mama deserves more love than I give to her." He embraced Pastor Kayode, moved back and placed his hands on his shoulders. He looked at him eyeball to eyeball. "That girl," pointing to Martha, "is very precious. She had gone through a lot and deserves to be happy. I want you to promise that you will make her happy."

"I promise Dad. I will."

"You are welcome to the family Son," he said, beating Pastor Kayode lightly on the shoulder.

Afterwards, the two men sat and discussed on politics. The women moved to the kitchen to prepare something for the house. Martha glowed with a new shine to her face, and Mrs. Aboderin walked with added springs to her steps. God is not man.

TWENTY

There were two weddings at Beulah between the months of October and December, in the year the weddings took place. The first was a societal wedding of the children of two big wigs in the Church. It attracted people from all walks of life. The Johnsons and the Williams outdid themselves in ensuring that, their children had the kind of wedding which would be the 'talk of the town' for years to come. Where money was sent with no thought for tomorrow.

The couple, Kike and Jide stepped into marriage like two sleep walkers. They were already bored of each other and were only fulfilling the desires of their parents, and the need to 'just get married' like the others were getting married.

There was no new thing to look forward to, except that both would legitimately bear the title of Mr. & Mrs. Although, they could now have sex with no restriction, that had become stale with years of secret copulation. Kike felt a danger looming over her soon to be home, like a sky that is pregnant with heavy rain. She felt like running away and never returning. She actually tried running away when it remained a week to the set date, but she had nowhere to run to. To make matters worse, she became privy to the information that Martha would be wedding Pastor Kayode in December. How and when they met she couldn't say. She learnt that they had already done the family introduction. Revd. Alhassan had briefly mentioned in one of his sermons that the most eligible bachelor in the Church- Pastor Kayode, would soon be getting married. Jokingly he said hence forth, no sister should disturb him again.

Kike felt a heavy pang of envy and a gnawing emptiness

within her. Her feelings became ambivalent. And though she was jealous, she at times wished she could be happy for Martha. She had the desire to go seek for forgiveness for the lies of years ago. She wished they could be friends again.

"How soon people forget things," Mrs. Johnson said on a Sunday afternoon after getting back from Church. "That stupid girl has suddenly become a celebrity because she's getting married to a Pastor. Parents are now taking their children to her to be counseled. I even heard she's running a program for 'after ones' like herself. Imagine! Revd. Bamiro even instructed me to incorporate her as a resource person into the program of the virgins' club."

Kike listened raptly to her mother. Her words made Kike more vexed against Martha, and she prayed something would stop the wedding. Something like Martha dying, or the Pastor changing his mind and leaving Martha stranded at the altar.

"And the senior Pastor is insisting on wedding them at the altar," Kike heard her mother say. "They will do a normal wedding with all the paraphernalia, despite the fact that the girl already has a child. Have you ever heard of such sacrilege? They want to defile the altar of God. Who does that?

"Madam!" her husband called. "Which is better? To join a repented and spirit filled single mother with her groom on the altar, or to join an unrepentant fornicator and a hypocrite, to an equally hypocritical groom like herself, at the altar?"

Kike looked sharply at her father and rushed into her room. Those words kept ringing in her ears even at the altar where she would be joined to Jide. They exchanged vows. The Pastor asked the groom to kiss his wife. A guest minister preached on the chastity of marriage. The choir sang. The virgins club presented an award of chastity to Kike. Afterwards, they went through the reception ceremony; smiling for the camera, giving fake testimonies of chastity, and dancing like there was no tomorrow.

The couple had their first fight the morning after the

wedding, on the day of their thanksgiving. Mrs. Johnson had called Jide on phone to remind him to call the Pastor, to tell him that he met his wife at home. Jide responded by cutting the phone on her. Surprised, Kike intervened, reminding him of their agreement. Jide replied that he was tired of her mother's manipulations and henceforth refused to be her puppet. He said Mrs. Johnson must be a witch for all her evil antics. Kike retaliated and called her husband a fool for insulting her mother, who had all along covered his misdeeds. She said if her mother was a witch, Jides's Mum must also be a witch, since both were friends. The statement earned Kike a star-producing slap and a red eye.

They were late for the thanksgiving service and received tongue-lashing from Revd. Alhassan. He said, marriage shouldn't make them draw back from being fervent in the Church. The new couple sat in the front row, flanked on both sides by their parents.

In the course of the same service, the banns of marriage for a wedding that would take place in the next two months was read for the first time. Martha and Pastor Kayode stood facing the Church, as the senior Pastor proclaimed their intention to become man and wife. He said that anyone that had a reason why they shouldn't be, to contact the Church authority.

Both would eventually get married in December, in a beautiful and Spirit-filled ceremony. The Pastor would prophesy into their lives, that their coming together would be a terror to the kingdom of darkness, and produce Godly seeds. They would end up becoming renowned ministers, with their ministry spanning across several countries in the world. They would later move to Australia with their children: Testimony, Timothy and Titus, from where the tentacles of their ministry would extend to the entire globe. But before then, on the day of the Williams' thanksgiving, as the Pastor announced their intention to become man and wife, Pastor Kayode stood confidently beside his intended.

Jide looked lost. He was scared to look up. At the same time, he sought for an eye contact with Martha, as she stood facing the

Church. She looked beautiful, with a kind of glow he couldn't explain. He wished she was his bride, and not the young but old cargo seated beside him. Since the incident of years back, there had been no much as one word between them. Martha looked at a point above his head into the congregation. The look said many things; that she had moved on, and he had no hold on her.

When Jide managed to look up, he caught Pastor Kayode looking straight at him. The look was so intent that Jide knew; that he knew. His wife to be had told him of Jide's complicity in her predicament of years back. Jide felt a nauseating sensation rise from within him. An internal heat that resulted in sweat breaking out all over him. Noticing his discomfiture, Kike fixed her palm into his for calm, but he pushed her away.

And then, he started hearing the Voice, which would not allow him to rest or take a breadth. In his head, in his ears, from within; the voice would always command him on what to do. At times it would be lone, while in some instances there would be multiple voices. All they do is, remind him of his guilt and past. Jide left the Church, hating his wife and his new marriage.

TWENTY ONE

It is always beautiful and glorious when couples discover themselves not before, but after marriage. When couples deny themselves of bodily pleasures and the desire to be intimate, until when they are spiritually and legally joined before God and man, as man and wife. Sex is good and beautiful, but is better enjoyed within the confines of matrimony. Even though the devil and his agents have filled the world with lies that make people lust abnormally and sometimes behave like lower animals without well-developed thinking faculty, the standard of God remains that the marriage bed should be undefiled.

A man that values a woman will do everything to help her keep her virtue and remain pure. A lady that sees herself as a princess will not allow any 'uncircumcised son of the philistines' to misuse her body. No matter the temptation, she wouldn't throw her pearl to be trampled by pigs.

Though their courtship period was short, Pastor Kayode and his wife entered into matrimony with a mindset to make it work. Starting from their wedding night, they began to erect a formidable structure on an already solid foundation. Despite the urge to know his wife, Pastor Kayode sensed that she needed a little more time to get used to him and feel relaxed with him. He wouldn't rush her. Whereas, she had become his for life. It wasn't easy controlling himself especially with the beautiful parcel that was waiting to be opened. Nevertheless, he waited until their third night together, when she was really 'ready' for him.

For a man that had never gone down with a woman and a lady whose sexual experience was that of teenage exuberance and then a rape, their joining was beautiful. All they needed to know they learnt together. A kind of tighter bond developed between them from their first time of copulation and they became inseparable.

True to his words, Pastor Kayode loved his wife like life itself. Martha reciprocated by loving her husband in return. She was submissive to him and both respected each other. They had no problem in settling their differences.

The Williams also settled in their new home. Jide discovered that they had too many differences. He would use every opportunity to castigate his wife. He became excessively hostile, critical and vindictive. That slap on the Thanksgiving Day became a daily routine. Jide often questioned if he had ever loved Kike, or if the love had just disappeared with the realization that they were now married.

Kike never enjoyed her marriage for a day because, Jide turned out to be a monster. Nevertheless, she suffered in silence, being too proud to seek for help. She continually prayed for God to give her husband a new heart. The fasting she wouldn't do before their wedding became a norm. Her prayer point was always that God should touch the heart of her husband. She became an overnight prayer warrior.

Jide and his wife still presented as a united and happy family to the outside world. They made it look as if they were enjoying the peace of matrimony. Often in anko, they post pictures of their happy family on the social media. Many young people would look at them enviously, and pray for a home like theirs. It was only Kike that knew of the fire that was burning under her clothe.

Discovering that Marriage is not only about sex after all, Kike's insatiable desire for sex disappeared with the birth of her first child. She craved for love and companionship, but all she had was a bed partner. A giver, who will drop any amount needed at home without batting an eyelid, but money cannot buy peace of mind. Kike had the good things of life, but had no peace.

She questioned God on why he had refused to answer her prayer. She sought his face for divine intervention but, it looked as if her heaven had been locked with a padlock and the key thrown into a turbulent ocean. Kike was desperate to do anything to have a happy home.

After a Bible study on a Monday evening, she waited outside intentionally to see someone. She had vowed to go to any length to redeem her home. She would start by seeking for forgiveness from Martha.

Martha padded out of the Church, bearing a heavily pregnant tummy before her. They met, greeted and Kike cleared her throat to speak. Suddenly, her courage failed her and she stuttered.

"Mrs. Williams are you okay?" Martha asked with genuine concern written all over her.

"I am okay," Kike replied in a subdued voice. She saw Pastor Kayode coming from behind and quickly turned her back to walk away.

Martha felt that Kike had wanted to tell her something. She stood starring after her as if she should follow her and make her to say her mind. Her husband met her in that position and whispered into her ear. "Are we okay?"

"It's Kike."

"What about her?"

"She was here a while ago. It seemed she wanted to say something, but changed her mind. She looked troubled. I just hope all is well with her."

"Hun! Mother in Israel," he teased. "Always concerned about everyone. I have told you to be worrying less, especially with your condition. We will put her family in our prayers."

"Is anything wrong with them?" Martha asked, looking up at her husband.

"I don't think all is well," he responded and took his wife by the hand. "We will pray for them."

Kike went home without bearing her mind. She started dodging Martha who was doing all she could to get close to her. Months later, she noticed that her husband had started talking to himself, and God help her if she dare ask him of what he's brooding about. He would curse her and curse her entire generation. She had no inkling that Jide was fighting a demon.

TWENTY TWO

Things went from bad to worse, before Kike got to know of her husband's inner struggles. That was when Jide stopped taking care of his personal hygiene, attending to his businesses, and eating her food. He would spend hours sitting at a spot and just murmuring. Alarmed, Kike ran to his parents.

Jide was first taken to a General hospital, from where he was referred to a psychiatric hospital; where he was diagnosed with schizophrenia. Kike's world came crashing down, the day it was confirmed that Jide had a mental disorder. Blaming her mother for pushing her into a marriage she would never enjoy, Mrs. Johnson replied that Jide is a cross she need to bear for the rest of her life. Kike said she never loved him after all, and her mother replied that she wasn't the one that aborted for him in the first. A heated argument ensued, and Kike told her mother that she hated her.

Their argument did not stop Jide's condition from deteriorating. One moment he would be fine, and the next he would go berserk. There were times he lost touch with reality, to the extent of defecating on himself. Kike could no longer tolerate him, so she bundled him to his parents. It became a hot news item that, Kike abandoned her husband at the time he needed her most. A clash between their parents was inevitable, and the Church had to intervene.

Revd. Bamiro; who would be retiring in a month time, summoned the two families to a meeting. Both families sat at opposite ends facing each other like two warring parties. Revds. Bamiro and Alhassan sat in between. Mrs. Johnson's unguided statement on why Jide shouldn't be in the meeting because he had lost touch with reality, was met with stiff opposition and renewed anger.

It was difficult settling a dispute between two sides that felt they knew better than the other, and hot words flew both ways. Revd. Alhassan's plea for calm was blatantly ignored. At a point, everyone wanted picking their belongings and leaving the meeting in anger. Then Jide shouted, and the atmosphere became quite.

He stood up as if a load had landed on him. With his large eyes in his shrunken face, it would take much persuasion for people to believe that, he was the same Jide that was a toast of all and sundry years back. His good looks had been replaced with the look of an insane man. As he made a move towards her, Kike shrank and hid behind her terrified Mum. Mrs. Williams gave the two a killing side ward glance.

Turning to the Pastors, Jide sank to his knee and burst into tears saying, "I heard the voice for the first time, the day we had our wedding thanksgiving."

"What voice?"

"The voice- in my head, in my ears, in my thoughts. He torments me and often bring other voices along.

Kike wanted to talk, but the Pastor made a sign with the hand for her not to.

"The voice came to subdue me, and I struggled to overcome him for years with sheer will power. He told me that there is too much guilt in me, that a guilty conscience is a fertile ground for its operations." Jide shouted, "I am guilty. I can hear him. I can see the picture vividly." He suddenly stood still, looking like someone in a trance, with eyes glazed. "The cry of my seeds that were not allowed to live, the cry of destinies that were aborted prematurely. They are many, too many." Jide wept like someone in uncontrollable pain.

"My seeds with Kike, Justina, Hauwa, Callista, Lovelyn,

Adaobi, and Romoke. We got rid of them; my seeds. They were aborted and wasted."

"But he said he had never been with a woman during their pre-marital counselling," Revd. Alhassan said to no one in particular.

"And she! She begged me."

"Who begged you?" Revd. Bamiro prompted.

Pointing forward, Jide burst into tears and shouted, "I want to see Martha."

"Martha?" Revd. Alhassan asked.

"Pastor Kayode's wife," Revd. Bamiro whispered and touched him lightly. "Relax! We are in for a big revelation. Thank you Jesus. What about Martha?" Revd. Bamiro asked Jide.

"I have to see her."

"You can't see her now."

"She came to me with joy radiating from her pores. She narrated her salvation experience, and begged me to give my life to Christ. I laughed at her. I mocked her."

"Pastor please stop him, he's deluded," Mrs. Johnson cried.

"Enough of the deception madam, please let him talk," Revd. Bamiro cautioned Mrs. Johnson.

"I stopped her from leaving. I slapped and kicked, until she became weak," Jide narrated. She fought with the whole of her strength, but I gagged her, carried and dropped her on the living room rug. I tore her pant in one sweep, and I raped her without mercy."

The picture looked so vivid, that all could not help but react.

The Pastors shouted, Jesus!

The fathers were too shocked to speak.

Kike whimpered into a hanky.

The mothers hid their faces in shame.

"Her blood stained my soul, where is Martha? Jide asked again.

"You can't see Martha now," the Pastor answered, but Jesus can wash your stained soul and deliver you."

"No! Jide screamed, 'I need to see Martha." He stood with a super human strength and dashed for the door.

All were too stunned to stop him in time. As if millions of demons were after him, Jide ran into the major road. A truck driver on speed couldn't apply his brake on time, and Jide was grinded to a pulp.

He died without giving his life to Christ. With years of Church services behind him, one wonders if those services would count for him in eternity. God cannot be mocked.

Kike became an emotional wreck. Graciously, she met the Savior. No longer under the influence of her Mum, she surrendered her life to Christ. She remained a widow all her life, doing kingdom work.

Mrs. Williams suffered a heart attack and died a year later. She died mourning her first son.

The Church members got to know about all that happened, and majority were eager to call Martha and give her the full gist. Martha and her Pastor Husband and lovely kids? They are far away in Australia, serving God among the whites, spreading God's word all over the world, and living peaceful and purpose driven lives.

Though Jide's death was traumatic to the Church, the event led to a much needed revival. Preaching his last sermon as the Senior Pastor, Revd. Bamiro challenged everyone to have a rethink about their relationship with God. The Church went into a period of solemn and intensive fast and prayers. Sinners became saved, backsliders retraced their steps, and chains were broken. It was the dawn of a new era.

Lest I forget, Mrs. Johnson was relieved of all positions in the Church. She totally lost relevance and cried of victimization. She stopped attending the Church, or any other Church. She would rather sit at the front of the house on Sundays, talking to an imaginary friend and criticizing passers-by.

ABOUT THE AUTHOR

Fagbemi Bosede

Bosede Fagbemi is an author, a mental health Nurse, a professional teacher, an entrepreneur and a mother of four lovely children.

She's an indigene of Ogbomoso, Oyo state, Nigeria, but grew up in Sokoto, Nigeria, where she developed the passion for reading and writing, right from when she was in the primary school.

She attended various schools which includes; Federal School of Psychiatric Nursing Sokoto, Natonal Open University, Nigeria and Federal University Dutsinma, where she's presently working for a Master's degree in Health Education.

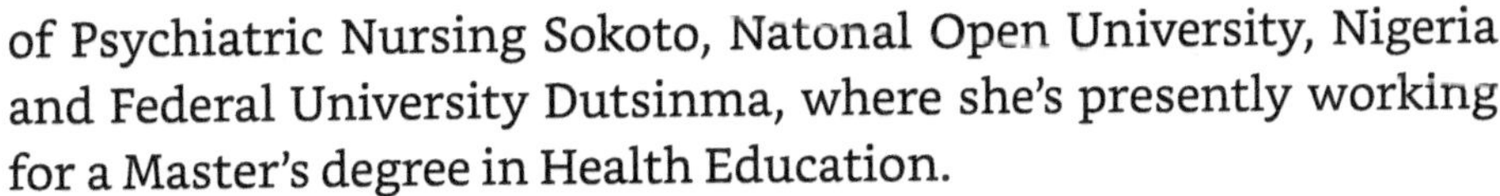

Bosede is an avid reader and a passionate writer. She enjoys writing on teenagers, youths, Family life and relationship. This is reflected in her books; Spoilt at Church, Sons and Daughters and Thirsty at the Riverside. Recently, she tried delving into investigative writing with the novel; The Searcher, which was a success and accepted by many.

Bosede lives and works in Katsina, Nigeria. She is married to
Adesina Fagbemi

BOOKS BY THIS AUTHOR

Sons And Daughters

Dinah is beautiful and intelligent, she's the first daughter to a small, poor and helpless widow. Mrs has suffered so much in life, first from the loss of her husband, and then the untold responsibilities place upon her by the society.

At the time of her husband's death, everything was taken from Mrs. Jacob, including the little that her husband left behind. She had no one to turn to for help, even as hunger threatened to send her and her four children to where her husband had gone. She would have to brace up and make the best out of a bad situation.

Mrs. Jacob wants the best for her children, especially Dinah. In her quest for succor to a life of abject penury, she decides to train Dinah in the University. The plan is for her to graduate, get a good job and lift the family out of poverty.

Dinah gets into the University and discovers that it is a different world from what she has always known. At the beginning, Dinah is like budding a rose. She is innocently beautiful, pure and full of vigor. She starts school with a gay spirit. She weathered the stress of registration and other activities. Before then, she had met Rhoda who became her roommate.

Everything looks strange to Dinah. The building, the activities and the people, especially the students. The way they act and speke isn't what she is used to. Her small and familiar comfort zone is world apart from the large world she met at the University.

Everyone wants to be seen and heard. Everyone wants to grab and own. Everyone wants to show their level of sophistication and open eyes. Everything is fast and different. So different that, Dinah starts feeling lost and disoriented- like Alice in the wonderland.

She weathers the storm of school life, but not without some drastic changes to her life and values. Almost at the point of graduating from the University, Dinah takes a step that places her life in danger. Would she survive? Mrs. Johnson is placed in a difficult situation. No one can quantify the agony of a mother, whose shining lamp is about to be snuffed off. What will Mrs. Johnson do to stop her hope to better life, waste away?

When people are handed responsibilities, they are expected to do well and prove their worth. Dr. Jay is a teaching staff in a private University. He has the habit of frolicking with female undergraduates and making life difficult for them. He does as he pleases, until the day he meets his Waterloo.
Before then, he makes a pact with Dinah, a pact that would see them travelling out of the school. Though he is the last person seen with Martha before the unfortunate incident that would put her life in danger, Dr. Jay would deny any involvement with her.

Another huge scandal would rock the boat of Dr. Jay's life, a scandal that would put all that he had ever labored for on the line. One wonders if he would escape the huge scandal that would result from his sexual escapades.

Kenneth is a son to a retired military officer- a tough man that doesn't mind shaming him, especially before his school mates and teachers. Kenneth's upbringing, coupled with his father's overbearing attitude, would gradually turn him into a social recluse.
Kenneth is forlorn, depressed and isolates himself, until the day

he meets Dampam; a fellow student and drug baron. Kenneth's life will never remain the same after the encounter.

The Searcher

Elder and Mrs. Thomas wants a good wife for their son, to them, a good wife is someone that is from a proper home and is well trained. The person must also be active in church and have a good report among the brethren. Tunde is their only son, the heir apparent to a vast business empire. They don't want a wife that would make him forget them and ruin what they had spent several decades building. Elder Thomas is an accomplished entrepreneur and a socialite.

Tunde would soon return to Nigeria from Abroad, for the wedding solemnization. He would readily agree with the choice of wife that his parents would make for him. He stands to get a lot by obeying them and giving a nod to all their demands including the need to marry a church girl.

Olaide is the choice of Elder and Mrs. Thomas, and they make their heart's intent known to the people that matter; Olaide's parent, the church pastor and Olaide herself. The pastor is vehemently against what Elder Thomas wants, first because match making is not biblical and more because Olaide is engaged to Martins. Olaide would have to make a choice of either staying true to her school teacher fiancée, or opt for a readymade man. Her mother preaches patience that a third man would come for her.

Martins is devastated that someone is planning to take his wife-to- be from him. He would fight tooth and nail to ensure that Olaide does not leave him. When Olaide makes her intent known to him, he vowed to deal with Tunde and threatened that if he wouldn't have Olaide, then no other person would have her.

Tunde eventually marries Olaide, in a talk of the town wedding ceremony. And on the wedding night, the unexpected happens. Was Tunde kidnapped or killed? How does one begin to unravel the mystery surrounding the disappearance of Tunde, the heir apparent to the Thomas dynasty? Eventually, Tunde's corpse is discovered.

The law enforcement agents begins a thorough investigation that will unravel many mysteries and open old and covered wounds. Olaide confesses that she has every reason to harm Tunde, but she did not. Tunde had committed an unpardonable sin against her just few days to their wedding. What will make a new bride, someone that has just been lifted from an average standard of living to a top notch life, kill her spouse on the wedding night? Could Olaide be saying the truth?

Lola is Tunde's ex-girlfriend, someone that he met in his days at the central University. Lola had willingly given herself to Tunde to be ravished. Tunde had deflowered her and left her in a limbo. He had suddenly disappeared when the news broke out that Tunde is involved in the killing of the sister of Scorpion - a dreaded cult guy. A month after Tunde disappeared, Lola discovers that she's pregnant. An effort to get rid of the pregnancy results in the loss of her womb. Could she the one that killed Tunde, after discovering that he's getting married to her sister's bosom friend?

Gloria is devastated that her best friend has lost her just wedded husband. She's even surprised that Lola and Tunde knew each other while at the University. Her earnest wish is for Tunde's killer to be found.

Scorpion, who has been vengeful for years is also a major suspect in the death of Tunde, but he claims that he has a strong alibi; he did not kill Tunde.

Someone claims that Tunde lived a rough life in the University, so it is his past that is haunting him. According to his baby mama, the reason for Tunde's predicament might just be tied to his past.

Steven; a passionate and committed detective, is saddled with the responsibility of getting Tunde's killer. Together with his ever active partner, Sharon, they will do all that is necessary to unravel the mystery behind Tunde's death.

Thirsty At The Riiverside

"My husband has never cheated on me. Why will he choose to tread the path of infidelity now?" That's the question that Katherine keeps asking herself, when she discovers a nude pIcture on her Husband's phone.

Katherine is married to Jayden and they are blessed with 2 children. They live happily, though not without the normal babble and squabbles between couple.

Jayden claims that the picture was sent in error. His wife choose not to believe him and concludes that he's cheating on her. That singular event, develops into something that becomes too big to be handled. Then, secrets begin to leak out; a secret business investment, a hidden side chick, a secretly done abortion, all threatens to pull down a once happy home.

Accusations and counter accusations begins to fly about. Old wounds are reopened. A separation seems inevitable. The children are left in a middle of a fight for right and supremacy.
Would the Jaydens be able to weather the storm? And what would be the long term effect of their action on the children?

Thirsty at the Riverside is a story for every couple at dfferent stages of marriage. it teaches why good communicaton s very important and why lttle issues could develop into a mountain that would serve as a barrier to family harmony.